HannaH WesT
in the Belltown Towers

HANNAH WEST

in the Belltown Towers

A Mystery by
Linda Johns

SLEUTH
PUFFIN

PUFFIN BOOKS

Published by the Penguin Group
Penguin Young Readers Group, 345 Hudson Street,
New York, New York 10014, U.S.A.
Penguin Group (Canada), 90 Eglinton Avenue East, Suite 700,
Toronto, Ontario, Canada M4P 2Y3
(a division of Pearson Penguin Canada Inc.)
Penguin Books Ltd, 80 Strand, London WC2R 0RL, England
Penguin Ireland, 25 St Stephen's Green, Dublin 2, Ireland
(a division of Penguin Books Ltd)
Penguin Group (Australia), 250 Camberwell Road, Camberwell,
Victoria 3124, Australia (a division of Pearson Australia Group Pty Ltd)
Penguin Books India Pvt Ltd, 11 Community Centre,
Panchsheel Park, New Delhi - 110 017, India
Penguin Group (NZ), Cnr Airborne and Rosedale Roads,
Albany, Auckland 1310, New Zealand (a division of Pearson New Zealand Ltd)
Penguin Books (South Africa) (Pty) Ltd, 24 Sturdee Avenue,
Rosebank, Johannesburg 2196, South Africa

Registered Offices: Penguin Books Ltd, 80 Strand,
London WC2R 0RL, England

First published by Puffin Books, a division of Penguin Young Readers Group, 2006

1 3 5 7 9 10 8 6 4 2

Puffin Sleuth ISBN 0-14-240637-6

Printed in the United States of America

To Kevin and Theo,
with thanks to Owen for getting me up at 5 a.m. to write

CHAPTER 1

YOU MIGHT THINK I'D FEEL A LITTLE TRIUMPHANT, HAVING GONE FROM homeless twelve-year-old to cushy downtown high-rise girl overnight. But mostly I was thirsty. This whole moving thing was getting tiresome, even when it meant moving up.

This time we really were moving up—up to the eleventh floor in Belltown Towers. It was my sixth move this year—six moves in sixth grade.

"Buck up, it's our last trip," Mom said. She put her laptop bag down on top of a wheeled suitcase.

"Water . . . need water," I said dramatically. I held up a plastic bag that was serving as transportation for Vincent and Pollock, my two goldfish.

Moving had become a ritual for Mom and me. We always saved a few things for the last trip. Our most precious belongings, Mom said. For her, that was her laptop computer, a painting by her friend Nina, and a small box of photographs (featuring yours truly). For me, it was my sketch pad, three big drawings I did last summer at the Y's Art for All camp, a wooden box of 120 color pencils, and a framed photo of me and my best friend, Lily, at the beach. And Vincent and Pollock, of course.

"Hold the elevator!" an older woman with a little dog called from the front door. Her dog reminded me of a silver-tipped version of Toto from *The Wizard of Oz*.

"I'm afraid there's nothing to hold yet," Mom said. "We're still waiting for the elevator."

The woman sighed. Her little dog plopped down into a sit, as if he were sighing, too. "This elevator is impossibly slow," she said. "I find it so inconvenient."

Uh-oh. My Snoot Alert went into active mode. Owen had told us that everyone in Belltown Towers knew one another. This woman was probably wondering what we were doing walking into her swanky building with armloads of stuff. She looked pretty swanky herself. Her salt-and-pepper hair perfectly matched her dog's coat, which somehow made more of a statement than my purple high-tops, which I'd thought tied in nicely with the purple Concrete Jungle logo on my black skateboard T-shirt. I had a sinking feeling that we wouldn't fit in at Belltown Towers at all.

But then the woman smiled. "Hello, dear," she said

to me. "It seems Ruff is quite interested in your drawings. Or your fish."

The little dog was sniffing and nuzzling me. I bent down to get some dog kisses while Mom rushed into her customary introductions.

"Hello, I'm Maggie West, and this is my daughter, Hannah," Mom said. She always tries to get to know people as soon as possible when we get to a new place. She says the more people we know, the more people will look out for us. "We're taking care of Owen Henderson's place while he's in Nepal."

"We're taking care of his fish, too," I added.

"Oh, of course," the woman said. "Owen told me about his house sitters. He also told me that a certain young miss is excellent with all kinds of pets, not just the aquatic variety."

"I love animals," I said, scratching Ruff on his belly. "He's a cairn terrier, right? Just like Toto?"

She laughed. "Yes, indeed. Not many people realize that Toto was a cairn. You must really know dogs." She looked at me again. "Dear, do you mind if I ask you something?"

Uh-oh. I knew what was coming now. I braced myself. She was definitely older than Grandma. Maybe even as old as GG (my great-grandma). She might be the kind who would ask, "Are you Oriental?" Lots of old people say "Oriental" for anything they think might have ties anywhere in the huge continent of Asia, including mu shu pork, sushi, and teriyaki chicken. But maybe she would be one of those people who just blurts out, "What are you?" because they can't tell someone from Korea or China apart. It makes me feel like a freak when someone asks me "what" I am like that.

The answer, in case you're wondering, is that I'm Chinese. But my mom isn't. She adopted me from China when I was six months old. It's not that unusual to be a girl from China adopted by non-Chinese parents, especially here in Seattle. Still, some people—usually the older kind of people—just aren't used to it.

But I digress. Mom brought me back to the present with a look that said, *Use your manners, Hannah.*

I took a deep breath and let it out, which turned out to be a bit of a sputter to blow some wisps of my ultra-straight hair out of my face. It's not the most sophisticated move, but it helps me think while I buy time. "Ask me anything you'd like," I said. I didn't really mean it. Clearly no one ever means it when they say "ask me anything."

"Well, dear, I'm having a little health trouble right now, and the doctor wants me to take it easy for a few days. I'm looking for someone to walk Ruff and make sure he gets enough exercise. Would you be interested in a dog-walking job? Owen highly recommended you," she said. "Of course, I need to make sure it's agreeable to your mother," she quickly added.

Mom nodded with a smile and I laughed. I hadn't been expecting that one at all. "I'd love to be Ruff's dog walker," I said. "And you can walk me, little guy," I said, scratching behind his perky ears. I reached into the back pocket of my shorts and pulled out a card. Some of my friends think it's totally dorky that I have business cards. But let me tell you, these things come in handy.

I handed one to the woman.

HANNAH J. WEST
PET SITTER, DOG WALKER, PLANT WATERER
AND ALL AROUND ERRAND GIRL
235-6628

"I can give you references, if you need them. And that's my cell-phone number. You can reach me there," I said.

The woman read my card and gave a little chuckle. "A cell phone, eh?"

"We're professional house sitters," Mom rushed in to

say. I think she was afraid I'd seem spoiled because I have a cell phone when the truth is that we're technically homeless. "I got a great deal on a family plan, so Hannah and I each have a cell phone. It makes it easy for our families to reach us when we're moving from house to house, with all our house-sitting jobs."

"Well then, that's a good idea. I think it's great for a young girl living in the city to have a phone with her," the woman said. "You can keep in touch with your mom and call for help if you run into trouble, which I'm sure you don't." She gave me a wink.

The elevator doors opened, and a man and a woman navigating a huge jogging stroller got off. "Sorry for hogging the elevator, Dorothy," the woman said.

Dorothy smiled warmly at them and said, "You certainly have your hands full." The three of us (four, if you count Ruff; six, if you count Vincent and Pollock, but I've noticed people don't usually count fish) got on the elevator.

"Oh dear. I neglected to introduce myself. I'm Dorothy. Dorothy Powers."

I thought I heard Mom gasp a little.

"You've already met Ruff, of course," Dorothy went on. "It seems my little companion has taken quite a liking to you, Hannah. Usually it takes a bit of a treat

to win him over, but it appears he instinctively under-
stands you're his ticket to walks in the great outdoors."

Ruff gave a little yelp when she said "walk." Just to
test him, I looked at him and said, "Walk?" He yelped
again.

"Sorry. Couldn't help myself," I said, feeling a bit
foolish for having teased my new canine client. I pushed
11 on the elevator panel, feeling the Braille spots above
it just to luxuriate in the idea of living up so high.

"Thirteen, please," Dorothy said.

I looked at the number panel. There were buttons
going up to twelve, but no thirteen. Above twelve there
was a button that said PH.

"It's the one that says PH, dear," Dorothy said.

"Why doesn't it just say thirteen?" I asked, pressing
the PH button for her.

"It's an old superstition," Dorothy said. "Even though
this is a new building, it's a little old-fashioned. You see,
some people used to be afraid of the number thirteen.
No one wanted to live on the thirteenth floor. So land-
lords would pretend there wasn't a thirteenth story.
They'd skip right from twelve to fourteen."

"But then fourteen would really be thirteen.
Wouldn't that be unlucky, too?" I asked.

"One would think so, if one believed such things.

I've been living on what is really the thirteenth floor for three years now, and I haven't had any bad luck," she said. "In fact, I wish they'd just call it thirteen and be done with it. Penthouse is a bit uppity for my taste, especially since the Belltown Towers calls both top-floor apartments penthouse. But I do love my apartment. You must come see it sometime. In fact, I have a new Hansen painting arriving today. I'd love to show it to you both."

We reached the eleventh floor, and Mom and I maneuvered our loads out into the hallway, trying not to get shut in the elevator doors.

"It was such a pleasure to meet you," Mom gushed.

I looked at Mom. She was practically beaming she looked so excited.

"It was lovely meeting you both," Dorothy called.

"You, too," I said. And I really meant it. I'd totally underestimated Dorothy. I'd been so caught up worrying about myself and whether she would call me "Oriental" that I almost hadn't given her a fair chance. My GG would say I was being ageist by assuming someone over seventy was going to be out of touch or, worse, as GG would say herself, "a culturally insensitive bigot."

"See you later, Ruff!" I called out just before the elevator doors closed completely.

I couldn't wait for my new dog-walking job. Not only

would it be nice to have a furry animal to hang out with downtown, I'd be making some much-needed cash.

"Ohmygod ohmygod ohmygod!" Mom said as she fumbled for the key to number 1105, Owen's apartment. I mean OUR apartment. "Do you have any idea who we just met?"

CHAPTER 2

AS SOON AS SHE GOT THE DOOR OPEN, MOM STARTED BUSTLING AROUND the apartment like a crazy woman. Which she is, sometimes. I mean, not really crazy. But she gets pretty excited over weird things.

I went straight into the kitchen. I needed to get Vincent and Pollock into a bowl of fresh water as soon as possible. All this moving every few weeks must be unsettling for the little guys.

"Do you have any idea who we just met?" Mom asked again.

Well, I thought I did, but now I was wondering if I'd missed something. "Who?" I demanded.

"Dorothy Powers!"

Sometimes it's so hard not to just blurt "Well, duh!" to a parent. But I speak from experience when I say that those two seemingly harmless syllables work overtime when it comes to annoying adults.

"Okay . . ." I stalled for time. The name didn't ring any bells to me. "So, who is she, besides the owner of my new client?"

"Dorothy Powers just happens to be one of the top three art supporters in Seattle! She has an incredible collection of art and a wonderful eye for new talent. If Dorothy Powers is behind you, you have it made as an artist," she said.

"Good. Maybe she'll discover me, and I'll be able to rent our old house back again," I said. My sarcasm went unnoticed.

"Owen told me she lived in this building. But I had no idea she'd be so nice. Or that we'd meet her our first day here. Our first hour here! Or that she'd invite us to her apartment! Did you hear her say that she's getting a new Hansen?" Mom fumbled in her purse for her phone. "I need to call Nina right away!" Mom headed out to the balcony with her cell phone. I whipped mine out, too. If she was going to call her best friend, then I'd call mine.

"If you're hearing this message, it means you should leave a message right after this . . . *beep*."

"Hey, Lily. Hannah here. If you want to call me, you can reach me in my downtown, totally happenin' condo. Later."

Lily had said she was envious of Mom and me being part of some schmaltzy *Lifestyles of the Rich and Famous* type of TV show, getting to stay in fancy houses and downtown high-rises. But I know she was just saying that to make me feel better, because the truth is I'd give anything to be back in our old house in the Maple Leaf neighborhood with my best friend just down the street, instead of six miles up the freeway.

And the rest of the truth is that I wasn't lying when I said we were technically homeless. I know, I know— it could be a lot worse. A LOT worse.

Here's the sixteen-word *Reader's Digest* version of what happened: Mom got laid off. We ran out of money. We started house-sitting instead of paying rent.

Here's the one-hundred-fifty-four-word version, for those who like a little more detail: Mom got laid off from her job at MegaComp. She tried to find a job at another dot-com company, but everyone was cutting back.

Someone with Mom's background—art history major, art critic, and writer—wasn't exactly in demand in Seattle's job market. She took a part-time job at Wired coffee shop and started freelance writing, but neither pays much. We had to make some serious cuts in how much money we spent. First we cut back on pizza deliveries. Then we canceled cable. We rented out a bedroom in our house to a college student. We had three yard sales. We held on as long as we could. Finally, we sold everything that wouldn't fit in our 1999 Honda Civic. One of Mom's old bosses at MegaComp let us stay at her house while she went on a four-week vacation. That was when Mom got the great idea of being professional house sitters, which is a lot better than being amateur homeless people.

Luckily, Mom is one of those people who knows a lot of people, including people who happen to be rich. Luckily, those rich people travel a lot—and they all like Maggie West. So it was natural for them to hire West House-Sitting Services to take care of their houses and pets while they bicycled around Scotland or went to cooking school in the south of France or climbed Mount Kilimanjaro or did whatever it is rich people do on their vacations. They head out to see the world; we get to stay in Seattle rent-free.

The best house-sitting gigs are the ones that last at least four weeks. This time, we'd totally scored. We'd be at Belltown Towers, complete with a view of the water, for nearly six weeks.

I took a look around Owen's apartment. I mean OUR apartment. It was a small one-bedroom with a million-dollar view (actually an $850,000 view, according to Mom, who said that's what Owen paid for this apartment, er, I mean condo, three years ago). I couldn't wait to tell Lily all about it. Living-room and dining-room windows looked out over Seattle's Elliott Bay and to Bainbridge Island. Even in the late spring there was some snow left on the peaks of the Olympic Mountains so that jagged white triangles towered beyond the water, making a backdrop that seemed almost fake because it was so postcard perfect. I headed out on the balcony and looked out at the water. I counted thirty-seven sailboats. A ferry belched its low horn, announcing it was on the move.

"That must be the Bainbridge Island ferry," Mom said. "We are going to have amazing sunsets. I think we're really going to like living here. Just look at all this!" She twirled around on the balcony and then leaned way over to look down. I felt like tossing my cookies.

"Um, where's the Space Needle?" I asked, trying to sound calm and perfectly at home on a tiny slab of concrete that jutted out nearly a hundred feet over the street.

"It's north and a bit behind us," Mom said. "You can't see it from here, not even if you lean way, waaaaay out." She swung her torso out and over the side. I shuddered. "Hmm . . ." Mom said. "I feel like I can see everything so clearly from here."

I opened my eyes and made sure she wasn't talking about my intense fear of heights. She was looking straight down to First Avenue, eleven stories below. I held on to the balcony railing, took a deep breath, and looked down. I gripped the railing even tighter. I felt a little dizzy. I stepped back, took another deep breath, and tried again. Nothing too remarkable, from my trying-not-to-barf-or-fall-off-the-balcony perspective. Just people walking on the sidewalks, a few people on bikes, and then a blur of purple and black as someone on a bike ripped around the corner and almost rammed into a jogger.

"That drives me crazy. Fast cyclists shouldn't be on the sidewalk, especially not someone from Swifty's," Mom said, heading back inside.

"Uh-huh," I replied. I had no idea what she meant, other than that speed-demon cyclists should ride on the street. I peered over the balcony railing again, just to prove I could. The purple-and-black-clad cyclist slowed down directly below us, hopping off his bike before he came to a stop. The large, flat package sticking out of the messenger bag that he had slung loosely across his back must have thrown him off balance a little, because his bike toppled to the curb against a parking meter. He didn't stop to pick up his bike or to lock it. It was like he was in perpetual motion. I had to stop looking down, or I'd be in perpetual throw-up mode. I settled into a deck chair on the balcony and refocused my energy on drawing the Olympic Mountains.

Sirens whined off in the distance. Then the sound got louder and louder, but I tried—unsuccessfully—to tune them out.

"Of course, we're going to have to get used to all the noise of living downtown," Mom came back out onto the balcony.

"It seems like they're coming right toward us," I said. I stood at the balcony's edge and dared myself to look down. A police car pulled up in front of Belltown Towers, and two uniformed officers got out. Another police car double-parked next to it, and then a solid blue car with a red light on top pulled in right behind the first one.

"What the heck is going on?" Mom asked.

"I don't know, but I'm going to find out," I said.

"Hannah, please don't get in their way," Mom said, following me out the apartment and down the hallway.

"I won't if you won't," I said. I stopped in front of the elevator and watched the numbers above the doors. Each floor number lit up as the elevator passed it: 7, 8 . . . the elevator was heading toward our floor and then right past it . . . 11, 12. Then it stopped at PH.

CHAPTER 3

"SOMETHING MUST BE WRONG AT THE PENTHOUSE," I CALLED TO MOM.

"We can take the emergency stairs at the end of the hall," Mom said. She tries to be the rational adult, but she's just as nosy as I am.

I raced toward the door that said EXIT in glowing green letters. I bounded up the stairs, two steps at a time, counting each landing as I went. If we were on eleven, the penthouse apartments were just two flights up. "Twelve . . . thirteen," I said out loud. There was an unmarked door at the landing, but there was still another flight of stairs.

"I thought thirteen was the top floor."

"Let's try that door," Mom said, right at the heels of my purple high-tops. "I bet that last flight goes up to a roof garden or something."

I hurled the steel fire door open and was ready to bolt down the hall, but I stopped myself. It seemed like I'd entered a new world. Or at least a new

17

building. Let me tell you, this top-floor hallway was nothing like the white-walled, blue-carpeted hallway down on eleven. Deep-piled, cushy carpet in a hunter green ran the length of the hallway, with a skinny red-and-gold plush Persian rug on top. The walls were painted a golden yellow orange, with gleaming dark wood trim. Oil paintings of landscapes and stuffy old-fashioned people hung on the walls in thick, ornate gold frames. I felt like I'd stepped into the den of an English lord's manor.

I shook myself out of my momentary awe and remembered why I'd raced up the stairs.

"Dorothy!" Mom rushed past me and toward heavy wood French doors that had PH-1 and D. POWERS etched onto a gold oval nameplate. A uniformed police officer at the door put a hand up as if to say *Halt*. So we did. Dorothy came to the doorway, her facing looking paler and older than it had just a half hour earlier.

"Maggie, Hannah, please come in," she said. "It will be good to have some friends for support right now."

The police officer stepped aside and mumbled "Go on in" to us.

Mom grabbed Dorothy's hand and walked her to a chair at the kitchen table. My mom is one of those people who can make anyone feel at ease, even during a crisis. Personally, I think she's a bit neurotic, but the rest of the world seems to find her amazingly calming.

I wasn't sure what to do. Follow Mom inside? Wait? Swap stories with the cop at the door? I stalled for time by looking down the corridor and checking out the scene. Right across the hall from PH-1 was its mirror image of double doors and a gold nameplate. Only this one said PH-2 and M. CHOMSKY on the gold nameplate. The door to PH-2 opened a crack, then quickly closed. Weird. Did someone know that I was watching? Or did I know that someone was watching? I decided to head into Dorothy's kitchen.

"I'm fine, Maggie. Really. But I did have quite a scare," Dorothy said.

"What happened?" I blurted out. Mom gave me a quick glare. *What?* I mouthed back to her. I mean, I can't be expected to be the most patient person in the world when a crime has just been committed. I have a high need to know EVERYTHING. Okay, so no one actually said there'd been a crime. But why else would three cars with sirens and lights be parked in front of Belltown Towers?

Dorothy looked up and smiled wanly at me, then turned her attention back to my mother. "The odd thing is that it seemed like Ruff knew something was wrong," she said. "I've never seen him react to any delivery person that way before."

"Delivery? What delivery?" I asked. Mom glared at me again. I wanted to put a fast-forward on this scene and find out what happened.

"It was like any other delivery, except for the way that Ruff was acting," Dorothy went on. "I'm sure the Swifty's messenger had no idea what he was delivering." She stopped to take a sip of water.

What was he delivering? I wanted to blurt out, but I held it inside of me.

"This must have been quite the surprise, then," Mom said. She was looking across the table to what at first glance looked like a framed painting. I did a double take. The canvas was blank.

"That's so weird," I said, avoiding Mom's glare. Geesh. How many times could Mom glare at me in five minutes?

"What does it mean?" I asked Dorothy, ignoring my mother's nonverbal admonishments.

"I have no idea," she said. "All I know is that when Ruff and I got back from our walk, there was a voice-mail message from Mimi Hansen saying she had a Swifty's bike messenger bringing me the painting I'd commissioned for the Honcho auction. No sooner had I heard her message than there was a knock on my door. I answered it thinking it might be you, Hannah, ready to take Ruff for a walk already."

"Someone knocked on your door? Isn't this a secure building, with an intercom and everything?" I asked.

"I'm not sure how the messenger got in, but that's not important," she said.

"I didn't know bike messengers worked on Sundays," Mom said.

"Oh, bike messengers work all kinds of hours," Dorothy said. "I run into them all the time making deliveries right across the hall."

"So, what happened to the painting that was supposed to be delivered to you?" I asked, trying to get this conversation back on track.

"It must have been stolen, although we don't know where or when," Dorothy said. "That's why I called the police."

"Um, Ms. Powers?" a police officer asked, as if on cue. "We have almost everything we need, but we'll need to interview your neighbor, a Mister . . ."

"Mr. Chomsky," Dorothy said. "Marvin Chomsky."

"Yes, Mr. Chomsky was the one who called it in," the officer said.

"I asked him to call. I was so shaken up when I unwrapped my painting. I was thrilled to finally have the new Hansen in my hands, but then I found this!" Dorothy said, gesturing toward the nonpainting. "But I doubt Mr. Chomsky can tell you anything. He never leaves his apartment. Messenger services bring him everything he needs."

"There's something else, Ms. Powers, if you don't mind," the officer continued. "Your dog. He seems to be in some sort of distress."

"Ruff? Distress? What's wrong?" I demanded.

"Perhaps I shouldn't have said 'distress,'" the officer said, a bit flustered. "He's under the bed and I can't coax him out."

"My reaction must have terrified him, especially once all the police arrived. Hannah, dear." Dorothy turned to me. "Would you go with Officer . . ."

"Officer Romano, ma'am," she said.

"Would you go with Officer Romano and see if you could bring Ruff out here? I think he'll come to you," Dorothy said. "Especially with this." She reached into her jacket pocket and gave me a little dog biscuit. "Dried liver," she whispered. "Just in case he needs added incentive."

I followed Officer Romano down a hallway.

"The dog's this way," Officer Romano said. "Did you say your name was Hannah?"

"Yes. I'm Ruff's dog walker," I said, trying to sound responsible. I didn't want to admit that I'd met the pooch less than an hour ago. "So, what kind of MO do you have on this case?" I asked. That's *modus operandi* in cop talk. I was a bit impressed with how effortlessly I rattled it off, especially since it's Latin. Roughly translated, it means "mode of operation," referring in criminal situations to how a perpetrator works.

"It's definitely not a standard case. And not just a prank, either. The substitute canvas suggests that someone knew exactly what was supposed to be in that package. Someone somewhere in this city has a valuable painting in their possession that they don't deserve to have," Officer Romano said.

"You've got to wonder how someone would have known what was being delivered to Dorothy, though," I said. I didn't pursue it because we were in the bedroom.

At least I think it was a bedroom. There was a large bed (my first clue), but there was also a sitting area with a table and stacks of books. Another part of the room had a yoga mat, a big blue exercise ball, and a bar for stretching.

I could hear Ruff whimpering under the bed. I crouched down to look. He started to growl, but then he relaxed.

"Hey, Ruff. Come here, little guy," I cooed. Nothing. I pulled out the liver treat and reached far under the bed to wave it as enticement. Ruff bolted toward me (or toward the liver), dragging his leash along the wood floor until he nipped the liver right off my open palm. I scooped up the little terrier. He was trembling like he was cold or scared—or both. I sat down on the floor and cradled him in my arms. "It's going to be okay, little guy. I'll stick with you," I said as I petted him. He seemed to relax in my arms. I set him on the ground, but he started to whimper as soon as I let go of him. "So it's going to be that way, is it? You want me to carry you?" I scooped Ruff up into my arms again. "This is Ruff," I said to Officer Romano. She gave him a scratch behind the ears. I had a good feeling about this cop, a feeling that was confirmed when I felt Ruff relax even more. "I'd better get him back to his human," I said, heading out to the hallway.

". . . no one but Mimi Hansen knew just how valuable this painting was," Dorothy was saying to my mom.

"Why would she let something so valuable out of her sight, then?" I prodded.

"Hannah . . ." My mom seemed to be warning me. Hey, we needed to keep Dorothy talking while details were still fresh, right?

Officer Romano tried to fight off a smile.

"Does this count as a burglary or a robbery?" I asked her. "I mean, I know it's a burglary if no one is there. And it's a robbery if people are on the premises when something is stolen. So, since we can't know exactly when the real painting was stolen, would you officially call this a robbery or a burglary? OUCH!" I cried as Mom reached out with her foot and kicked me.

"We haven't released an official statement from the Seattle Police Department yet, but I think we're safe to call this an art theft," Officer Romano said.

"Right. It's a definite theft. Maybe even a heist," I offered.

Mom grimaced. "Hannah," she said, with more than just a smidgen of warning in her voice. It was sort of like she was saying "Don't be so dramatic." If she were an icky mom on a TV show, she would have said something like "You read too much" or "No more Crime Network for you."

Officer Romano had gone out into the main hallway for a phone call. She came back and looked extremely serious. "I need to tell you that there was a theft at the Mafune Gallery around the corner yesterday," she told Dorothy. "I'm not saying that the two cases are connected, but I thought you should know before the newspapers get ahold of this, since paintings by this same artist . . ." Officer Romano flipped through her notebook. "Yes, since both paintings were by this Mimi Hansen, I'm sure the media will blow this all out of proportion."

"Oh dear," Dorothy said. "Why on earth would someone target Mimi Hansen?"

Then she collapsed.

CHAPTER 4

I TOOK RUFF DOWNSTAIRS AND OUTSIDE. HE HAD TOTALLY FREAKED out when Dorothy collapsed, and he started barking like crazy. I held Ruff while Mom helped Dorothy until we knew she was okay. She'd blacked out, something she said happens every once in a while because of some kind of blood-pressure something or other. I wasn't really paying attention. My mind buzzed with thoughts of this strange art heist. I had lots more questions, but the adults had dismissed me and the dog to another walk.

The police had already interviewed Dorothy before Mom and I got up to the penthouse, but clearly I'd brought up some excellent points. Then Officer Romano told me my services could be put to better use if I did my job as a dog walker.

The important thing was that Dorothy was okay. And that Ruff got some time outside.

Click, click, click.

I heard a clicking sound on the sidewalk. It sounded like someone was wearing baseball cleats and walking really fast. Almost like a horse trotting.

"Come on, boy, let's go this way," I said, leading Ruff around a corner.

Wham! All of a sudden I was on the ground. And someone or something had plowed into me. But what? I looked up.

"Watch where you're going!" I snapped from my sprawled position on the sidewalk. Ruff was squished under my right leg.

"Are you okay?" A guy in his twenties in full cycling gear—helmet, gloves, Lycra bike shorts—was looking down at me. He held out a hand to help me up. Ruff started to growl, but then stopped.

"If you move that fast without a bike, I'd hate to run into you when you were on a bike. . . ." I said, standing up and brushing off the seat of my shorts.

My voice trailed off. Mr. Bike Guy did a one-eighty and headed back the way he came before I could finish talking.

Click, click, click.

So that's what was making that noise. Bike Guy had those kind of cycling shoes that snap right into bike pedals. Lily's dad said they were great for riding a bike, but totally obnoxious and awkward when it came to trying to walk without looking like a dork. Bike Guy looked a little dorky as he sped up into race-walking mode. He darted around the corner at Battery Street, but not before I read the word *Swifty's* on his purple-and-black T-shirt.

"That was weird," I said to Ruff. Weird that Mom had just said something about Swifty's. And definitely weird that in my first hour in my new neighborhood I'd already got up close and personal with the concrete.

A car horn honked. I leaped back from the curb, pulling Ruff with me. I didn't need to add a car accident to my list of mishaps today. A little white convertible pulled up to the curb right in front of Belltown Towers. A woman with blond hair and big dark incognito movie-star sunglasses jumped out and ran to the front of the building. She pressed one of the buttons that calls up to the apartments.

"Officer Romano," I heard over the intercom.

She must be calling the penthouse. I moved a little closer.

"I'm here to see Dorothy Powers," the woman said. She spoke as if the police officer upstairs were a maid. And how come she didn't wonder why a cop had answered the intercom? Maybe this woman was an investigator. She sure didn't look the part, but maybe she was working undercover or something.

"Your name, please?" Officer Romano's voice cackled over the intercom.

The woman sighed a bit impatiently. "Mimi Hansen," she announced.

Mimi Hansen! Wow. She didn't look at all how I expected an artist to look. She looked more like a TV talk-show host or something. She wore a short leopard-print skirt and a tight button jacket that matched it. On top of her head was a leopard-print hat, kind of like a beret you'd wear on Halloween if you were pretending to be a French artist. Her feet were strapped into the highest-heeled and pointiest-toed shoes I'd ever seen. Aren't artists supposed to look funky and poor, even if they aren't poor? Not this one. That's for sure.

I heard some garbled noise coming back over the intercom, and then the front door buzzed open. "Hold the door, please!" I called, pulling Ruff with me as I high-tailed it toward the open door. Mimi Hansen looked me up and down, stopping at my bony knees that were now scuffed up thanks to my run-in with the sidewalk. No matter what she thought of me and my bare legs, she still let me in. Sometimes being a kid has its advantages.

I smiled my most innocent smile.

"Hi. I'm just taking Ruff back up to his owner. You know, Dorothy Powers," I said.

"Oh, right. I thought that mutt looked familiar," she said, pushing the elevator "up" button.

Mutt?

"Actually, Ruff is a cairn terrier. A purebred. Not a mutt," I said importantly. I don't know why I felt I had to talk to her. There's just something so uncomfortable about standing around waiting for an elevator with someone.

"Of course it is," she said. She started jabbing the "up" button again, as if that would make the elevator come any faster.

Ruff crouched down. A low little growl came out of him.

She reached down to pet him. "Muff and I are old friends, aren't we, Muff?" she said.

Muff?

Ruff sprang up and started yipping. He jumped from side to side. He crouched down and growled again. Then he nipped at her hand.

"What's with that dog? Get it away from me!" she screamed.

The elevator doors opened. Ruff jumped inside and assumed his tough-guy crouch-and-growl position again. Mimi took a hesitant step forward. Ruff's growl got louder.

"You go on ahead," she said as she backed up. "I think I left something in the car." She cleared her throat. "Tell Dorothy that Mimi Hansen is on her way."

It sounded like an order. Geesh. How many times did this woman need to announce herself?

CHAPTER 5

"IS EVERY DAY AT BELLTOWN TOWERS THIS EVENTFUL, PUPPY?" RUFF didn't answer me, but he seemed to be settling down again. By the time the elevator reached the penthouse floor, Ruff was full of sloppy kisses and contented tail wags.

Dorothy and Mom were still sitting at the kitchen table.

"I think we're done for the day, Ms. Powers," Officer Romano said. "Please call us directly if you hear or see anything suspicious. Or if you think of anyone who might have wanted to do something like this to you."

"Oh, I'm supposed to tell you that Mimi Hansen is on her way here," I said. Mom looked at me curiously. "What?" I said to Mom. "I met her downstairs." I'm not sure, but I think my mom looked slightly impressed that I'd already met this artist person. I decided not to add that she'd been bossing me around.

"Oh, thank you, Hannah. And thank you, Officer Romano, for being so kind," Dorothy said.

"I hope you can relax with your guests now," Officer Romano said. "I'll certainly keep you informed as we investigate your case." She bent down to scratch Ruff behind his ears. He licked her hand happily. She was just out the door when a human whirlwind made her entrance.

"Oh, Dorothy! I was so worried about you! Are you all right, darling?" Mimi Hansen rushed into the apartment, teetering on her ridiculously high-heeled shoes. She said "darling" so it sounded like "dahling."

Ruff started growling again.

"I'm fine, Mimi. But someone stole your painting on its way here!"

"What?" Mimi gasped.

"It's true. I'm just so sick about it. I was so excited to see *The Blue Principle* again before the Honcho auction, but when I opened the package, I saw this . . . this . . . this . . ." Dorothy gestured toward the empty canvas.

"What?" Mimi practically shrieked. She appeared to have an extremely limited vocabulary.

"Weird, huh?" I interjected. "You've got to wonder how someone even knew what was inside the package, since it was wrapped in plain brown paper and all."

"No one even knows about that painting but you and me," Mimi said, speaking directly to Dorothy, as if I hadn't uttered a word. "Why would someone target it?"

"It seems this thief has a good eye," Dorothy said.

"Yes, I see your point," Mimi said, suddenly composed. "That particular painting is exquisite in its play of light. It is a fine example of the quality of my work. Your thief has impeccable taste." She actually tried to chuckle. It didn't work.

"Yeah, but how did the thief know what painting was inside the package?" I said. "The switch must have been made before the bike messenger picked it up to bring over to Dorothy."

"I believe my young friend Hannah is correct," Dorothy said. "Oh! Forgive my bad manners! Mimi, these are my new neighbors, Maggie West and her delightful daughter, Hannah West. Maggie and Hannah, this is Mimi Hansen, one of the most promising artists on the West Coast."

"I've heard so much about your work," Mom said, holding out her hand. Mimi hesitated and then extended her hand for a limp nanosecond handshake. It seemed she was about to dismiss us when Mom added, "I write for *Art Voice*."

Mimi turned on a high-beam smile for Mom. At least I think it was a smile. The corners of her mouth were turned up, but it didn't reach the rest of her face. "Maggie, perhaps you already know that

Dorothy is donating one of my creations to the Honcho auction. What you might not know yet is that Dorothy's generous spirit inspired me to create a second piece for the auction, the painting that was stolen. It's called *The Blue Principle*. It's part of a series I'm doing. One of the other pieces, *Principally Blue*, is right there," Mimi said, gesturing like a game-show model toward a big blue painting hanging on Dorothy's dining-room wall. I hadn't paid much attention before, but now it drew me into its swirls of blue. It was a painting of nothing, and a painting of everything. I stared at it. I felt like I could fly and swim at the same time. It truly was beautiful. Extraordinary, really.

"I didn't realize that was yours, Mimi," Mom said. "I didn't see your signature on it."

"I haven't signed it yet," Mimi murmured.

"I thought artists signed their work as soon as they finished," I piped up.

"Not always," Mimi said quickly, with a pointed glare toward me. At least she'd acknowledged that I was in the room.

"That's one of the many things that makes both *Principally Blue* and *The Blue Principle* so special!" Dorothy said. "It's such a clever idea that Mimi had for the Honcho auction."

"What's Honcho?" I asked, having heard about this auction twice in just the past few seconds.

"It's an auction that raises money for the arts in Seattle," Mom said. "Many arts groups couldn't survive without money from the Honcho auction."

"Exactly!" Dorothy said. "It was such a surprise when *Principally Blue* was delivered to my apartment. After I'd admired it for a few minutes, I noticed it didn't have that characteristic Mimi Hansen signature that she's so well known for. I thought that was puzzling, so I called Mimi right away."

Mimi shifted in her chair. She recrossed her legs. I flinched reflexively, afraid that one of those high-heeled shoes would spear me.

"Mimi pretended it was an oversight at first." Dorothy laughed. "As if she would actually forget to put her signature on a painting like this."

"Well, I can get forgetful while in the throes of my creative energy, you know. . . ." Mimi trailed off.

"That's when Mimi told me her big surprise! She hadn't signed it on purpose. That way, we can create excitement at the auction because Mimi will be there to sign this painting in front of a crowd of some of the wealthiest people in the city."

"How unusual," Mom muttered.

"It's actually quite a brilliant idea I had," Mimi said, attempting once again to chuckle. It sounded more like an evil vampire's laugh. "In fact, it was such a good idea that I decided to create the other painting. Of course, I didn't sign that one, either."

"Maybe that's why someone wanted to steal it," I said.

"Because the thief didn't want the auction to make money?" Dorothy asked.

"Because of my brilliant idea?" Mimi asked.

"No. Because if it didn't have a signature, how could you prove it was a Mimi Hansen? If it's such a good painting, and I'm sure it is," I hurriedly added, "then someone else could take credit for it and sell it."

Dorothy and Mom stared at me.

Ruff licked my hand.

Mimi glared at me again. She was getting good at it.

CHAPTER 6

BY TWO O'CLOCK ON SUNDAY, I'D MOVED INTO A NEW APARTMENT, GOT a job as a dog walker, met a famous artist, almost witnessed an art heist, and started a new investigation. I was hungry.

I grabbed my sketch pad, and Mom and I headed out to explore our temporary neighborhood. Belltown is part of downtown Seattle, but it's just north of the big businesses and tall glass skyscrapers. Condos, coffee shops, restaurants, bakeries, coffee shops, apartments, art galleries, coffee shops, and bars line the streets of Belltown. Did I mention coffee shops? Seattle is a bit coffee crazed, and it's not just because Starbucks HQ is here. Anyway, Belltown is the kind of neighborhood where you can eat your way around the world, with Japanese, Cuban, Vietnamese, Spanish, Chinese, Greek, Mexican, Italian, and French restaurants—but no fast-food joints—all within an easy walk.

"Is there some kind of zoning law here? Like, 'There must be one art gallery, one restaurant from each continent, and two coffee shops per city block,'" I said.

"Make that each side of the street for each block, and I think you've summarized Belltown pretty well," Mom said. "So, what will it be, the Noodle Ranch or the Noodle House?" We were right in front of the Noodle Ranch, and we would have had to go all the way across the street to get to the other Thai noodle restaurant. The Noodle Ranch it was.

When you're technically homeless and your mom is a waitress, spending money at restaurants isn't exactly high on the list of things to do. I never knew noodles could taste as good as they did at the Noodle Ranch. And talk about affordable! I suggested doing a taste test and heading to the Noodle House for dinner, but Mom said we still needed to watch our budget. "Besides, there's lots to do back at our apartment," she added.

It feels weird to call it "our" apartment because it's really Owen's. That night I curled up on Owen's eggplant-colored leather couch and looked over the sketches I'd started earlier that day. I'm what's known in my family as an OCS (obsessive-compulsive sketcher), which Mom says is an artistically accepted cousin to OCD (obsessive-compulsive disorder). She also says it might work well with my crime investigation, since OCD doesn't deter San Francisco detective Adrian Monk on the TV show *Monk*. He can't pass a lamppost without touching it. I can't pass a lamppost without sketching it. Compulsive sketching pays off, though. I have lots of material to shape into my newest graphic novel venture, starring a brilliant young girl of Chinese descent on the trail of a mysterious art thief.

"Hannah," Mom interrupted me from my drawing state. "I just got a call from Wired." She sat down on the couch next to me, clutching her cup of herbal tea. I could smell Monkey Jasmine. Mom may work at a coffee shop called Wired Café, but she never drinks coffee. Just tea. "I can do an extra shift tomorrow, but I'll need to be there by five-thirty."

"In the morning?" I whined.

"Yep. I'm really sorry, but you know we—"

"—need the money," I finished for her.

She hugged me, spending a little extra time, like she was going to say more. Then efficient Mom Mode took over, and she spread out three Metro bus schedules on the coffee table. "I think you know all the north-end routes, but here are schedules for the 72, 42, and 7."

Mom went over my bus options while I tried to turn off the continuous recording in my head:

I hate being homeless . . . I hate being homeless . . . I hate being homeless . . .

I know, I know, I know: I'm not truly homeless. Technically homeless, yes. But out on the streets? No. Sleeping in a car? No. Living under a bridge? No. And yet it's so close.

Every once in a while I like to have a little pity party with yours truly as the guest of honor. That's what I did our first night in Belltown Towers. Not even a million-dollar view (or an $850,000 view, in this case) could get me past feeling sorry for myself. But cable TV is the perfect guest at the Hannah West Pity Party.

I put my sketch pad away and started flipping channels. Total score. Owen had more cable channels than our last house-sitting job had offered. I flipped quickly from Channel 2 all the way into the eighties. "Come on, come on . . . Yes!" Channel 85 was TCN, The Crime Network, twenty-four hours of crime right in your home. I loved this channel. The Crime Network had the real-life investigative shows with detectives and scientists. It also had lots of police dramas like *CSI* and *Law & Order*, funny ones like *Monk*, plus super old detective shows like *Columbo*.

"Now, this is educational television," I said, settling in to rewatch the end of a *Monk* episode. Aside from building my logic and deduction skills, my crime-TV watching keeps my math skills sharp. According to my calculations, I currently have a 92 percent success rate solving crimes. On television, that is.

I watched another episode of *Monk*, one that I hadn't seen yet, and actually forgot to keep feeling sorry for myself.

Nothing like solving a mystery to cheer me right up.

Hannah West's TV Crime Solving Success Rate: 94 percent.

CHAPTER 7

"GET UP AND SHAKE YOUR BOOTY! SHAKE YOUR BOOTY!"

Ever notice how hard it is to get up on a Monday morning? That's why I, Hannah J. West, employ a little obnoxious disco helper.

"I said: GET UP and shake your booty!" I hit the "snooze" button on my disco alarm. I knew I'd pay for it later.

Five minutes later: *"Did you not hear me? I said: GET UP and SHAKE YOUR BOOTY!"* The disco queen was louder and screechier, accompanied by a mini-disco light show and rotating silver mirrored ball. I've really got to move that thing across the room so that I absolutely have to get out of bed the first time it tells me to shake my booty. Especially when it's my first day in a new place and my mom is already at work.

I hit the street at 7:20, heading to Third and Pine to catch the number 72 bus. Perfect timing.

Mom was right. I really was a pro at this. Ever since I was little, she and I had gone all over the city of Seattle on Metrobuses, from the Alki lighthouse in West Seattle (number 66 downtown, then transfer to the number 56 or 37; total trip time fifty-two minutes from our old house) to the swimming beaches at Lake Washington (number 2 from downtown for twenty-one minutes), and just about everywhere in between. She didn't let me go by myself until sixth grade, and even then she made absolutely sure that I knew what I was doing. I did. Of course. And now it was totally worth it. Being able to get around the city on Metro meant I could keep going to Cesar Chavez Middle School, no matter where we were house-sitting.

I got off six blocks from school. I didn't want any snoopy or snooty parents to see me on a city bus. No matter how bad middle school can be, at least Chavez isn't completely miserable. It's the north end's AA school. Officially, that's for "Alternative and Accelerated." Everyone at Chavez is considered "advanced." Whatever *that* means. You have to have certain test scores or recommendations from teachers to go there. You also had to live north of the Ship Canal. We used our old address in the Maple Leaf neighborhood for my school assignment. We were superlucky there, too, because the people renting our old house kept our mail for us.

I was a block from Chavez Middle when a little white two-seater convertible with a BMW emblem screeched past me and pulled over to the curb. I had a flashback to Mimi Hansen parking in front of Belltown Towers yesterday. Uh-oh. It *was* Mimi Hansen. But she wasn't getting out here. A blond girl about my age stepped out of the passenger side. The door hadn't even closed all the way when Mimi accelerated away.

The girl looked around, as if checking out who was watching her. She glanced at me, then looked quickly away. She was the kind of girl who *wanted* to be watched (especially getting a ride to school in a spiffy car like that). But she also looked nervous, as if she *didn't* want anyone to see her. She was heading toward the front doors of Chavez, just like I was. She turned around and glared at me again, as if I were following her. Well, I was, technically. But only because I had to get to school before the final bell. If she was starting at Chavez, the New Girl Alert would spring into action, and we'd know all about her by lunchtime. This girl was one mystery I didn't have time for.

The first bell rang, and I headed into school and straight for homeroom.

"Hey," I said to Lily.

"Hey back," she said. She didn't even look up from

her book, but she wasn't being rude. She was just being Lily. And that means preoccupied with a story. She unclipped her bangs on the right side and reclipped them, then did the same thing on the left side, managing to turn a page in the middle of clipping. Both of us play with our hair—I'm a hair twirler and she's a hair twister—and both of us are trying to get out of the habit. Today Lily had her shoulder-length straight brown hair in two pigtails twisted into buns. She says if she restricts her hair she won't play with it as much. The result is that my fair-skinned, blue-eyed, freckled Irish friend looks like a cross between a leprechaun and Princess Leia from the original *Star Wars* movies. But I'm not about to tell her that. Her right hand reached up for her hair clip.

"Put the clip down," I whispered in a mock-cop voice. "Walk away from the clip and we'll all be okay."

She looked up at me. Glared up at me, actually. Then back to her book.

"Who done it?" I asked, flopping my messenger bag down next to her desk.

"Not sure yet," she replied, still not looking up. Lily was on an Agatha Christie mystery binge. She'd gone on a mystery-reading jag last summer, starting with Sir Arthur Conan Doyle and then moving on to Dame

47

Agatha. She was on a mission to read every single book by Agatha Christie.

I peeked at the cover of her book: *Murder at the Vicarage*.

"What's a vicarage, and who was murdered there?" I asked.

Lily still didn't look up. "A vicarage is like a church. I don't yet know who murdered the magistrate. I daresay it wasn't the vicar, but I'm not sure I trust Griselda. However, I do believe it was someone in the parish."

"Huh?"

"Hannah, you really need to learn to speak British if you want to keep up with me, old chum," Lily said with a bloody good accent. "Now leave me alone so I can get to the bottom of this before Miss Marple."

"Don't forget our local art-thief mystery, Miss Shannon," I said. Lily and I had e-mailed back and forth yesterday, so she was up on the action at Belltown Towers.

"Listen up, people," Mr. Claussen, our homeroom teacher, called. "We've got a few announcements, and then we'll take the rest of the period for quiet time. You can read, do homework, sleep, or draw." He looked right at me at the end, which I assume was for the drawing suggestion, as I'm not much of a classroom sleeper.

"It's so unfair," I whispered to Lily. "An entire school

year will go by without us having a class together, and we don't even get to talk in homeroom half the time." The cruel scheduling program didn't even give Lily and me the same lunch period.

She sighed dramatically and went back to Miss Marple, and I worked on a female sword-wielding manga bike messenger until the bell for second period rang.

"Note you?" I queried.

"Note me," Lily confirmed. "I'll note you back."

We were on a retro covert communication mission. Everyone at Chavez was into instant messaging after school and text messaging between classes. I'd read this article about students in Japan who were actually using paper and pencil to scribble notes to one another, then using their camera phones to take a picture, and sending the note to a friend. The whole idea was so preposterous that Lily and I vowed to be devoted paper-note correspondents.

We headed out the door. I raced down two flights of stairs and along a long hallway to the art studio. The one good thing about my schedule this year was that I'd finally gotten into Drawing/Painting 3. Getting to draw first thing in the morning was some consolation for not having the same lunch as Lily. I sat down at my regular table and got out my colored pencils. I am totally in love with the Prismacolor pencils my grandma gave me for my last birthday. They're not at all like the ordinary colored pencils you get at the drugstore or Office Warehouse. These are considered "artist quality," with wonderful pigment. It's easier to control your color and line with really good pencils. And thanks to Grandma, I had a deluxe box of 120.

"Let's get started," Ms. Murdoch said. She expected us to be ready to work as soon as the final bell rang.

"You can sit right there by Hannah," Ms. Murdoch said. I hadn't been paying attention until she said my name.

I looked up as that new blond girl sat down next to me at the table. I smiled. She didn't.

"This will be your permanent seat for the rest of the quarter," Ms. Murdoch told her.

Great, I thought. This girl didn't seem terribly friendly. Besides, I'd gotten used to having the whole table to myself.

The new girl smiled at Ms. Murdoch. Then she mumbled, "Just great."

At least I hadn't said anything out loud. Or had I?

"Um, I'm Hannah," I said.

"I'm Jordan," she said.

"Where are you from?"

"Bellevue," she answered. And that one word said it all. Bellevue is a suburb on the other side of Lake Washington. Superrich people live in Bellevue, including Bill Gates, one of the guys who started Microsoft—who, in case you haven't heard, is the richest person in the world.

"I want you to start right away sketching this still life. Don't worry about colors or details at this point, of course," Ms. Murdoch said, looking at me since I already had my colored pencils out. "Concentrate on the forms and their relational sizes." It was an odd assortment of things for a still life—a small African-style drum, a clay vase with a single tulip, and an old-lady kind of teacup and saucer with dainty pink roses around the rims. The combination did not look particularly intriguing or attractive. I wasn't sure if there was some weird hidden symbolism in these objects.

"I hope we don't have to talk symbolism," Jordan said under her breath.

I stifled a laugh. Maybe this new girl from the suburbs wasn't too bad after all.

"I like your highlights," she said. "They remind me of Vermilion. Or maybe Carmine Red."

Interesting. This girl didn't say "red." She used

specific Prismacolor pencil hues. Most people just say, "I like those reddish streaks in your hair."

"Actually, I think of this more as Crimson Lake," I said. "Number 925," I added, to see if she really knew her stuff. She smiled, so I guess she did. I was going to ask why she'd switched schools so close to the end of the year, but the teacher was heading toward us.

"Jordan, I'm so thrilled to have you in class," Ms. Murdoch said breathily. "I'm a huge fan of your mother's work. I couldn't believe it when I read in the *Times* this morning that someone stole one of her paintings from the Mafune Gallery and then another one en route to Belltown Towers."

I stared at Jordan. "Is your last name Hansen?" I asked.

"No, it's Walsh," she said.

"But Mimi Hansen—"

"—is my mother," Jordan finished for me. She had that steel-eyed look that said, *You want to make something of it?*

"Oh, wow. I just met her yesterday. She's really famous. I saw this painting she did called *Principally Blue*. It's gorgeous."

"Yeah, right. I'll bet it is. She's sure some artist." Jordan clearly wasn't interested in talking with me. Or maybe about her mom.

CHAPTER 8

THE BELL RANG. I PACKED UP MY THINGS AND HEADED TOWARD THE DOOR.
Jordan followed me out. I was still trying to get my head around all of a sudden having a new girl in school who just happens to be the great Mimi Hansen's daughter. But then I turned into Hannah West, Helpful Girl and Ambassador of Kindness to new students. "Do you need help finding your next class? I can give you the lowdown on the best lunch line, too," I offered.

"Are you both the school artist and tour guide?" Jordan asked. She said "artist" so it sounded like "artiste." Then she added, "By the way, where did you get your Prismacolor-inspired streaks?" She smiled while she talked and walked. At least, the corners of her mouth were turned up, but her face wasn't really going along with it. I suddenly saw the family resemblance between Jordan Walsh and Mimi Hansen. Twenty-four hours ago, I had never even heard of Mimi

Hansen. Now she was everywhere, including a younger version right beside me in the halls of Chavez Middle.

I stopped and Jordan practically screeched to a stop beside me. Was she making fun of me and my hair? I'd have to cut ties with her now before she commented on my vintage Urban Surf T-shirt or managed to find something wrong with my jeans.

"Listen, Jordan, I'm not exactly sure why we're talking about Prismacolor names or my hair, but if there's something I can help you with at Chavez, let me know," I said.

"Ladies! Welcome!" Mr. Ogata came out in the hall. "Your presence is requested inside my fascinating class," he said. "We have a lot to go over today."

Jordan followed me into Mr. Ogata's room. Just my luck. Jordan Walsh was in social studies with me, too. And that meant she was an honors student.

I copied our homework assignment from the board, but I didn't hear a word Mr. Ogata said for fifty-five minutes. All my brain cells were fired up and fuming, but also swirling and muddled. How could someone I didn't even know act so weird around me? I tried to look like I was paying attention to Mr. Ogata, but I doubt I was very convincing.

• • •

Finally, social studies was over. But my time with Jordan Walsh wasn't. It dawned on me that if she was in social studies with me, she'd also be in honors language arts. Jordan got up to leave.

"Not so fast," Mr. Ogata said as he came over to her. "I'll try not to be hurt that you're so eager to leave me. But this is a two-hour honors block. Check your schedule, Ms. Walsh, and if it says 'Honors Language Arts,' then you're staying here with the rest of these inquiring minds." Jordan made a show of pulling out her schedule and looking it over, then she gave a big sigh and settled back into her seat.

"You all have five minutes to talk softly, stretch, do some yoga or mental gymnastics," Mr. Ogata said. "And then I'll be introducing you to the wonderful Mary Wollstonecraft Shelley."

I used my five minutes to draw a retro note to Lily. I wasn't sure if the sports car, the glammed-up image of Mimi Hansen, and the doodles of Jordan in my first three classes of the day would mean much to Lily at this point, but it was fun to draw.

Jordan stayed in her seat across the aisle from me, but she left my mind within minutes of Mr. Ogata telling us about the world of a young girl named Mary

Wollstonecraft, who, by the age of twenty, had written and published one of the most famous novels of all time. We had only thirty minutes left to start reading that novel, *Frankenstein*. I could barely stop when the bell rang for lunch.

I shoved my books into my locker, pulled out my sketch pad, and headed to the lunchroom. I got a bean burrito, carrots, and chocolate milk from the lunch line. I get free hot lunch, thanks to Mom's low-wage job. I've read in some books that getting hot lunch is a sure sign that you're poor. It's not that way at Chavez Middle School at all. You get to pick from three main things every day—like pizza, burritos, taquitos—and usually one of the choices is decent. You "pay" by punching in your secret code. No one knows whether you used a hundred-dollar bill, your dad's American Express card, or a free pass to pay for your food.

Even all the TC girls (The Clique girls) buy hot lunch. It's too much of a hassle to bring a lunch. Chavez Middle is a "model environmental school." If you bring your lunch, every container you bring has to be reusable. No brown bags that get tossed into the garbage. No Ziploc bags unless you plan to reuse them. And let's face it: We sixth graders don't have time to wash out our Ziploc bags. That would take away from the wonderful social lives we enjoy.

Yeah, right.

I sat on a stoop on the side stairs with my sketch pad. I needed to get Jordan Walsh and Mimi Hansen out of my head. So I put them on paper again.

By the time the bell rang for sixth period, Jordan had turned into Medusa. I must say, snakes growing out of her scalp looked eerily natural on her. I added it to my other pictograph note to Lily and added, "Guess who is in three of my classes?" and then folded the note into tight triangles until it was less than one inch big. On my way to sixth-period Japanese, I slipped my retro paper note through one of the slots in Lily's locker.

CHAPTER 9

"YO, HANNAH! WAIT UP!" LILY CALLED TO ME.

I slowed a little but kept walking. "Hey, Lily."

"Why are you in such a hurry to get to the bus?" she panted.

"Just keep walking. I'm trying to avoid someone. I'll tell you later," I mumbled. "But keep talking and walking. Like we're having a fascinating conversation."

Lily did some loud fake laughter. "Oh, that is too funny! What did she do next?" That's my best friend. A born actress. I could count on her to switch into character at a split second's notice.

"Did you have to make it a *her*?" I grumbled. "I just hope she's not around."

Lily had no idea who or what I was talking about. But she didn't miss a beat. "You mean you saw your cousin and her boyfriend right in the middle . . ."

That got some looks from the kids around us. We were moving like a pack out to the bus lines.

"Okay, okay. Good job. You saved my face." I laughed back to Lily.

"Yeah, well, no problem. But when we get on the bus, you're telling all."

Getting on the bus is part of my daily charade of being Hannah Jade West, the middle-class girl who lives with her mother in their comfortable two-bedroom home in Seattle's Maple Leaf neighborhood.

In the winter, Mom wanted me home by 5:00 or 5:30 because it got dark so early. That meant getting off the school bus, picking up the mail at our old address, and heading back on Metro to wherever we were house-sitting. But now that it's almost summer, it stays light until eight o'clock or later at night. I could hang out with Lily until dinner and still make it the seven miles back downtown with plenty of daylight left.

Lily and I had planned to put on our sleuthing hats during the bus ride home, but first I needed help figuring out why Jordan had acted so strange to me.

"Do you think she got kicked out of her old school?" Lily asked.

"That seems pretty extreme," I said, mulling this over. "But it's definitely weird that she'd switch schools so close to the end of the school year."

"I'd throw a fit if my parents tried to get me to move to a new school right now," Lily said.

"Maybe she needed a clean start."

"She needs a code name," Lily said. "Got one?"

"Haven't thought of one yet," I said. "Let's see . . ." Lily and I have code names for practically everybody we ever need to talk about. That way we can talk freely—usually—about people. The trick is to find codes that aren't too predictable, but not so complicated that we can't remember them ourselves.

"JW or IJW for Icky Jordan Walsh." Lily started brainstorming.

"No obvious initials. I'd bet a hundred dollars that her friends call her 'J-Dub,'" I said. "That is, if she has any friends."

"Oh! I have it! Mini Mimi!" Lily started singing "me me me" scales, like an opera singer warming up. I joined in with "Mini me me me, Mini me me me" until we both collapsed in giggles.

"I. Have. An. Idea." Lily gasped, trying to stop laughing. "How about NJ, for Nasty Jordan? We don't actually know that she's nasty, but we've got some early indicators."

"Enj?" I tried sounding it out instead of using the initials. "Enj," I said again.

"Perfect! Easy to remember. Rolls right off my tongue."

We got off the bus on Northeast Eightieth Street and Eighth Avenue. Jamie, the bus driver, winked at me. Uh-oh. Did that wink mean Jamie knew I was just pretending to live up in Maple Leaf?

"Okay, Lily. Do you want to go to my house or your house?" I said loudly as I clambered off the bus.

"Can we go to mine first?" Lily said, just as loudly. Geesh, can you see why I love this girl? She's a true best friend. She should get an Academy Award for Best Actress Supporting Hannah West's Game of Deception.

If Jamie the bus driver was paying any attention to us, I thought we'd given pretty good cover.

We headed to Lily's house. First on the agenda: Stress Dancing. We turned up the stereo in her family room superloud and jumped around. After three songs, Lily turned down the stereo, and we headed for home-work and cookies.

At five o'clock, Lily's dad and little brother, Zach, got home. I started getting my stuff together to leave.

"Can you stay for dinner, Hannah?" Lily's dad asked. "I'm experimenting with a new dish tonight. It's rich with antioxidants and fiber."

"Thanks, Dan, but I can't," I said hurriedly. I'd

forgotten that Lily's dad was creating new recipes and writing a cookbook for his organic food co-op. His working title for the book was *Life Gets Better with Kale*. No matter how much I like the Shannons, I didn't feel like learning what kale was. "I'm going to head downtown and meet my mom. It's easy this time. We're staying at the Belltown Towers."

"Wow. Pretty fancy. Do you have a view?" Dan asked.

"Yep. Eleventh floor corner unit, full view. And it's all ours—at least for six weeks."

"It seems like I just read something about the Belltown Towers in the *Times* this morning," Dan said.

"News at the Belltown Towers? Let's see . . . robbery, art heist, and all kinds of high-end intrigue. We're in the thick of it," I said.

"The paper said the robber pulled a fast one, switching a blank canvas for an authentic Hansen painting that was about to be delivered to some wealthy art patron. That sounds like a smart villain. I love Hansen's work," Dan said.

"Really? You do? Why?" I really wanted to know. What was it about this artist that had everyone's eyes lighting up?

"Well, I guess I don't love all her stuff," Dan said.

"Then again, that's what's so great about her. You can't peg her style. Almost every piece is different. She's got tremendous range."

"Range?"

"Some landscapes, some abstract, some soft and subdued," Dan said. "I could go on and on about it—"

"But you won't," Lily cut him off. "Because Hannah has to go. Right, Hannah?"

"Right." Thank you again, Lily Shannon. I'd decided that I'd had enough talk of Mimi Hansen for a while.

CHAPTER 10

I SPRINTED DOWN TO EIGHTIETH STREET. TIMING IS EVERYTHING. And my timing is perfect—at least when it comes to Metro buses. It's like I have this weird mechanism inside that's perfectly tuned in to Seattle city buses. Sometimes I'll be sitting in class and I'll look at my watch and think, *Hmm . . . 1:32 P.M. The number 6 will be at Third and Pine right about now.* I have the schedules and routes memorized for sixteen different buses. Best yet, I always get to a bus stop right on time.

Like now. I got to the stop on Northeast Eightieth Street just as the 66 came into view. I hopped on and found a window seat for the ride downtown. Here's another little tip I've learned in my Metro riding experience: Always wear headphones. No one bothers you if you look like a kid listening to loud music. My miniplayer was out of batteries. In fact, I didn't even have my mini with me. But with my earbuds in place, I pulled out my sketch pad and looked around for a victim . . . Er, I mean, I looked for a fellow passenger to draw.

I'll give him a try, I thought to myself. The guy sitting two rows ahead and across the aisle from me looked kind of familiar, in that brown-haired kind of cute older guy (midtwenties) kind of way. Too old for me and too young for my mom, but I had my eye on him for another reason. He had that five o'clock shadow thing going on. Drawing people is hard no matter what, but perfecting the shadowing needed for facial hair is an extra challenge. One of the characters in my graphic novel has two days' growth of beard. I needed to work on stubble. I decided to manga-ize this guy, drawing him Japanese comic style.

I got so engrossed in my drawing that the bus was all the way south of the Pike Place Market and the Seattle Art Museum before I noticed I'd missed my Stewart Street stop. Darn it. I pulled the cord to signal the bus driver someone wanted off at the next stop. I stuffed my sketch pad in my backpack and headed to the front of the bus.

The guy I'd been drawing hopped off ahead of me and took a bike off the bike rack in front. He started walking his bike down the street.

Click, click, click.

This time I recognized the sound. Bike cleats. The same sound I'd heard outside Belltown Towers yesterday. It made perfect sense that he'd make that noise. He had a bike, after all, not to mention black cycling shorts, a purple hooded sweatshirt, and one of those bike messenger bags slung across his chest.

Come to think of it, both the thief at Belltown Towers and Bike Guy had messenger bags like that. So, maybe the thief was a bike messenger? Okay, wait. I needed to remember that old phrase "Don't shoot the messenger." The bike messenger was just delivering a package. Someone had probably switched the bags before the messenger even started pedaling off on the delivery. Right?

Or was my imagination getting a little overactive?

Maybe not. The bike guy from the bus took off his sweatshirt. He was wearing a purple-and-black Swifty's bike-messenger jersey.

Maybe I wasn't so crazy after all.

I did what any normal twelve-year-old sleuth would do.

I pulled out my cell phone.

"Lily! Where are you?" I said to her answering machine. "Hannah here. I'm hot on the trail of a bike messenger. Could be the same one I saw outside Belltown Towers . . ."

Beep.

Lily picked up the phone.

"Do you have any idea how many bike messengers there are in Seattle?" she asked.

"No, but this one is wearing a Swifty's shirt. And so was the one at Belltown Towers. Are you going to tell me that's just a coincidence?"

"Do you have any idea how many bike messengers work at Swifty's and wear those jerseys?" Lily asked.

"Well, how many of them ride the bus instead of a bike?"

"Maybe the ones who are riding the bus downtown to get to work," Lily offered in a patronizing voice, like she was explaining the absolute obvious to me. "Some of those Metro buses have bike racks in front. My dad and I put our bikes there when we took the bus to the Arboretum last summer."

"Stop with the logic and the family stories," I whined. "What if *this* guy is the art thief? Maybe he's working with the guy who knocked me over yesterday? Like his accomplice, or a lookout or something."

"Well, then, my paranoid little friend," Lily said slowly, "you might as well indulge yourself in your art-thief theory and follow the guy. Go ahead. Follow him!"

Of course, I was already following him while I talked

on the phone. He was conveniently heading north, walking alongside his bike, heading in the same direction I needed to go to get home to Belltown Towers. When he leaped on his bike and started pedaling, I had to hold myself back. Just because there was a slim, slight, minuscule, teensy-tiny chance that the thief was a cyclist didn't mean that this cyclist was a thief. Lily was right. Downtown Seattle was teeming with cyclists. Bike messengers wove in and out of traffic on weekdays, not to mention all the people who commuted to their jobs on bikes.

Before I knew it, I had lost him.

I looked around for the nearest bus stop and realized that I was at Second and Pine, close to Nina's studio space. I might as well see if Nina was around. Nina, my mom's best friend, let me keep an easel and some supplies in a corner of the studio. She shared the studio space with a bunch of other artists, but she said I was welcome to work on my own stuff as long as she was there. I was so close, I decided not to call first. I'd stop by, like people are always doing in books and on TV shows.

When I got to First Avenue, I looked up at the fourth floor of the Stimson Building. Lights were on in Studio 4, Nina's studio space. I was about to buzz the studio when . . .

Click, click, click.

Man, was my mind destined to endless echoes of that clicking sound? It was getting to be like an annoying song that gets stuck in your head, like those high-pitched girls singing "Tell me more, tell me more" in that song from *Grease*. Only this time the cleats were thundering—and they were real—and they were coming down the stairs inside the building. The door swung open.

"Thanks, I was about to buzz," I said, catching the door, as the same bike guy from my bus came out. No time to exchange pleasantries, apparently. My hunch about him being a thief evaporated. He was just an ordinary Swifty's bike messenger, picking up an ordinary oversize package at the Stimson Building.

He jumped on his bike and took off remarkably fast. It was remarkable because he was also carrying a large flat object wrapped in brown paper. Sort of like what I'd seen yesterday when I was on the eleventh-floor balcony at Belltown Towers.

CHAPTER 11

I GRABBED THE DOOR TO THE STIMSON BEFORE IT CLOSED SO I COULD run up to the studio without buzzing. If Nina wasn't there, I could at least leave her a note. I sprinted two steps at a time to the fourth floor. The dimly lit hallway had five doors leading into what realtors advertised as "loft space for artists." Nina shared a space with a bunch of artists I'd never even met.

The door to Studio 4 was open a crack.

"Nina?" I called as I walked in.

Music came from a boom box in the corner, and I thought I heard water running in the back. Maybe Nina was there washing out brushes.

"Nina? It's me, Hannah," I called again.

A tall man with dreadlocks came out of the washroom.

"Yes? Nina is not here," he said. He had that kind of Jamaican/Rasta-sounding voice.

"Oh. Sorry," I said. "The door was open, so I thought

I'd see if she was in here working. I'm a friend of hers."

The man didn't say anything.

"Nina lets me hang out here sometimes and do some work. That's my easel over there," I said, pointing to a corner.

He moved over in front of some paintings lined up against the wall. "Nina is not here," he said again.

I guess that should have been my cue to leave. But noooo. . . . Something caught my eye. My artist's eye, as Mom would say.

"Are these yours? These are fabulous," I said, walking toward the three small canvases behind this guy. Maybe I should have been on guard about being in a building with a total stranger. But he wasn't really a stranger if he worked with Nina. She and her studio mates were always supercareful about who they shared their space with. Besides, as I stared at the three paintings, I was getting pulled into a world of swirling blues. I couldn't look away. I stepped closer, and scenes of alleys and streets unfolded in the myriad of blues. Each painting was only about a foot wide, but it was full of details, giving it the impression of being much larger. "The play of light in this one is so intriguing," I said. Eww! I sounded like a hoity-toity art person. But the words *play of light* were jumping around in my mind. Where had I heard that phrase recently?

The man shuffled from foot to foot.

"Um, my name is Hannah West," I said. I held out my hand. "Like I said, I'm a friend of Nina Krimmel's. Actually, she and my mom, Maggie, are friends. She just tolerates me."

He shook my hand quickly and let go. "I am James," he said.

"I love your work. I feel like I've seen it before. . . ."

"It is not ready to be seen yet," he said.

"I guess that's why you haven't signed these three," I said.

"I do not mean to be rude to one of Nina's friends, but perhaps it is now time for you to leave," he said. Was it my imagination, or was James a little nervous? I know a lot of artists are perfectionists (a trait that hadn't appeared in me yet) and didn't want anyone to see their work until it was absolutely perfect. James's paintings looked pretty darn perfect to me.

"I'm sorry to have bothered you while you were working," I said. "Is it okay if I leave Nina a note?"

"Yes, yes. Leave her a note. And then I think you should go," he said.

I turned to a fresh sheet of paper in my sketch pad

and did a rough sketch of one of James's blue street paintings. I hoped it looked like I was writing. James went back to the sink area. Then he came back and draped a paint-splattered sheet over the three paintings.

"These are not ready to be seen," James said yet again. "Come back some other time, when Nina is here." He went back to cleaning brushes.

I drew a superquick sketch of James. I left a note folded for Nina.

> Nina,
>   I stopped by. Can I come paint some night this week?—H.W.

"Has your work been in a gallery?" I called out to James. "I feel like I've seen it before."

I heard a woman's voice in the hallway.

". . . I'm at the Stimson Building to see what James has ready to go. I need at least one more from him, plus whatever we get at The Factory on Friday night. . . ."

It was one of those annoying cell yellers—the kind of person who walks around with a cell phone constantly glued to her head, talking loud. What's really annoying is that you get only half the conversation—the cell yeller's half—when you eavesdrop. It's terribly unsatisfying.

"The messenger is on his way. . . ." the cell yeller said, but then her voice dropped and I couldn't hear. Something about "making a witch" or "making a switch." Whatever.

The cell yeller was getting louder and the door to Studio 4 opened wider.

Mimi Hansen walked in.

CHAPTER 12

"WE'LL TALK LATER," MIMI SAID INTO HER PHONE. SHE FLIPPED IT SHUT with a snap.

"James, I thought you'd be alone. I thought we had an understanding that *your* work was highly secretive," Mimi said. She glared at me, even though she was talking to James, with absolutely no sign of recognizing me from yesterday.

"This is a friend of my studio mate," James said hurriedly. "She stopped by to leave a note for Nina. She was just about to leave." He grabbed the note from me.

"I will give this to Nina," he said. He looked at Mimi and said quietly, "You don't have anything to worry about."

"You'd better hope I don't," Mimi said. She put on her sunglasses, even though we were inside. She wrapped the belt of her Granny-Smith-apple-colored trench coat tighter and turned up the collar. If she'd had a fedora, she would have totally looked like a cartoon spy. Well, except for the bright green coat and the fuchsia turtleneck underneath. She wasn't exactly inconspicuous.

James beckoned me to the door.

"Tell me, have we met before?" Mimi asked. Her eyes looked me over, up and down.

"Um . . ." I was about to remind her of Dorothy Powers's apartment when her cell phone rang again.

"Yes?" she said into the phone as she turned away from me. And I am not making this up, but she waved as if she were dismissing me, as if she were shooing me out the door. "No, no. He's on his way with the real one. On a bike. Trust me. It's faster this way. Traffic is terrible. . . ." Mimi went toward the back of the studio to keep talking.

"I will make sure that Nina gets your note," James said. He held the door wide open for me. I can take a hint.

What the heck was Mimi Hansen doing at Studio 4? And why did she mention a bike?

"Mimi Hansen was at Nina's studio?" Mom asked. We were eating Trader Joe's burritos in Owen's dining room. The sun was heading down toward the horizon in the west, making the lower sky a warm mix of pinks and oranges that shimmered in the water of Elliott Bay. Dinner with a view. "Did Mimi see any of Nina's work?"

"Dunno," I said as I took a bite of my burrito. "It seemed like she was there to see James. They wanted me to leave."

"James? The cute dreadlocks guy? Hmm . . . he just got a space in Studio 4," Mom said. "Maybe she's mentoring him or something."

"Mimi Hansen doesn't exactly seem like the mentoring type," I said.

"Did you see his work? It's pretty fabulous. He does those bright geometrics based on body organs. It sounds weird, but his paintings are amazing."

"Maybe you don't really know this guy, Mom. Because the James I met was doing street and alley scenes, not livers and kidneys. They were this intense blue. One looked like Post Alley down at the Pike Place Market. Another one reminded me of Pioneer Square. Wait. Let me show you. I mean, I can't really show you the paintings, but I did a quick sketch of the alley that looked like Post Alley."

"An interesting departure," Mom said as she studied the sketch. "Maybe James ran out of organs. And you're right; that's Post Alley. That looks like the door to Kell's Pub. Really, Hannah, this is quite good." She clicked on the TV. Even with Owen Henderson's five hundred premium channels, Mom switched to the local news on KOMO–4 to see what her college friend Mary Perez was covering. If Mary was reporting, it was usually something juicy.

"Let's go to Mary Perez for more of the story," the news anchor said.

"Oh, good. Perfect timing," Mom said.

"I'm outside the Von Hiers Gallery in the downtown neighborhood of Belltown, where a thief just stole two paintings by celebrated artist Mimi Hansen," Mary said.

"That's right around the corner!" I said excitedly.

"Shhh! I want to hear this," Mom said.

The camera had started with a close-up of Mary Perez. Now the view widened to show the "Von Hiers Gallery" sign and the front of the gallery.

"I spoke with gallery manager Cleveland Mathis a few minutes ago. The paintings disappeared some time shortly before six-thirty this evening. The two stolen paintings were part of Hansen's latest *Seattle Streetscape* series. There are two things that make these paintings special. First, they're rather small, just thirteen by eleven inches. Second, each painting has a distinctly different style, use of color, and overall look. In fact, the only thing that these paintings have in common, art experts tell me, is that they are by Mimi Hansen, and they do, in fact, have that distinctive 'Mimi Hansen signature' on them. The Von Hiers Gallery had six of these Hansen paintings on display. After today's theft, only four are left."

Mary Perez paused. I knew that meant someone was talking into the little earpiece in her ear, telling her something. Mary told me how hard it is to talk into the camera at the same time as someone is talking into your ear.

"A large painted canvas wrapped in Kraft paper was delivered to the Von Hiers Gallery just before it was discovered that two Hansen paintings were missing. Since the gallery was not expecting a delivery, the package has been turned over to Seattle police for processing," Mary said, pausing briefly again as if listening to someone update her.

"Do you think the mystery package delivered to the gallery might be like the one Dorothy got?" I asked. Mom shushed me so she could keep watching the news.

Mary resumed talking. "Two days ago, a Hansen was stolen from the Mafune Gallery. And yesterday a privately owned Hansen painting never made it to the delivery destination at Belltown Towers downtown." Mary paused again, then said, "I'm told that Mimi Hansen herself just arrived at the gallery."

The camera shot widened a bit again, and there was Mimi Hansen. It had been only an hour since I'd seen her at Nina's studio, but she was wearing a completely different getup. She had a monotone thing going on now with a sleeveless gold turtleneck and lots of thick gold chains. Her face and hair kept the golden thing going to the top of her head, making all of her shimmer for the camera.

"Man, she's everywhere these days," I murmured.

"Ms. Hansen, do you have any insight into why someone would be targeting your work at three separate crime scenes this week?" Mary asked.

"It's evident to me that people in Seattle are just now beginning to realize the brilliance of my work," Mimi said, looking directly into the camera instead of at Mary. She grabbed the KOMO microphone out of Mary's hands. "I've been heralded internationally for the depth and variety of my artistic work and my interpretation of the world around us. No one can imitate my style because no one ever knows what Mimi Hansen will have next month, next week, or even tomorrow. My work in progress is always kept very secretive. I am constantly working, creating my vision. I am, as some say, inimitable. No one can reproduce my extensive body of work. The only option for an artful thief would be . . . to steal it." Mimi stopped dramatically. She gazed into the camera and slowly shook her head. "It's a shame, really. My work inspires so many people, but I didn't expect it to inspire criminals."

"Barf. Could her ego be any bigger?" I asked Owen's flat-screen TV.

Mary snatched the microphone out of Mimi's hands.

"That was local artist Mimi Hansen. Two paintings by this *prolific* artist were stolen just a half hour ago from the Von Hiers Gallery downtown."

Mom laughed when Mary said "prolific." Just because someone—like a writer or an artist—produces a lot, it doesn't mean that the person is necessarily good. But somehow people seemed to think it was some kind of compliment. I was pretty sure that Mary hadn't meant it favorably.

On the TV screen we could see a wider view. Mimi was storming off, shooing away people who tried to talk to her. The camera kept backing up, showing more of the street and the people gathered around the art gallery. Mary did her regular TV-reporter sign-off: "We'll have an update for you on the eleven-o'clock news. Live from downtown Seattle, this is Mary Perez for KOMO TV. Back to you, Kathy. . . ."

And that's when I saw them: Not one but two Swifty's bicycle messengers were in the background.

CHAPTER 13

"YOU'RE CRAZY," LILY SAID INTO THE PHONE.

"That's irrelevant to the case," I said. "We've got to see why bike messengers are swarming all over the Seattle art scene."

"Swarming? Listen, Sherlock West, they're pedaling. That's what bike messengers do. As the offspring of a messenger, I know these things," Lily said.

I'd completely forgotten that Lily's dad, Dan, had worked his way through graduate school as a bike messenger. He always said it was the greatest job he ever had.

"Hey, could you ask your dad about it? You know, if any of this seems weird to him?"

"I can ask him, but Hannah, it might have been a little weird on the weekend, but today's a regular workday."

"Aren't most offices closed by now? It's after seven," I pointed out.

"Still, it could be just a—" Lily started to say.

"Don't say it's just a coincidence," I interrupted. Lily was silent. I guess that was exactly what she was going to say. Either that or she was busy swallowing the Chee•tos she hoards in her room to make up for her dad's daily organic dinner specials.

I knew Lily couldn't resist the appeal of a real-life mystery any more than she could resist a Miss Marple mystery. She was on the case, as far as I was concerned, and I could count on her. We made plans for her to spend the night at Belltown Towers on Friday.

"I need to get back to my trig homework. Mrs. Olson is killing me with this endless homework. Night after night after night. She piles it on," Lily said.

"Trig? What are you talking about?"

"I'm practicing what I'm going to say to my parents so they'll leave me alone and let me read in my room. They're back on their No TV on Weekdays thing. They're terribly eager to play a rousing game of gin rummy right now."

"Got it," I said. "Lily, do you even know what 'trig' is?"

"Not exactly. But I think I'll sound more convincing if I say I have trigonometry to do."

Jordan Walsh (or "Enj," as I'd decided to call her) wasn't in class the next day. Not that I'm an attendance taker or anything. It's just that it would be hard not to notice whether the new girl was there or not. It would also be hard not to notice that Zac Mason, Ryan Steinberg, and a few other guys were obviously disappointed by Jordan's absence. Geesh. You'd think that 51 percent of Chavez Middle School—the 51 percent that was female—was invisible or something, the way the guys were talking about Jordan. Already they were referring to her as J-Dub. Lily and I had been crafty to go for Enj as her code name.

I rode the school bus home with Lily, but she had to get to a clarinet lesson, so there wasn't time to hang out with her. I headed to her house anyway. It's part of my cover. You see, if it seems like I'm just hanging out with my best friend, maybe no one will notice that Mom and I don't live in that neighborhood anymore. You wouldn't think anyone would care, but there's one pesky kid on the block who could blow it for us.

"Hi, Hannah," Dira called out to me.

And that was the kid.

"Hey, Dira," I called. Dira's mom was on the Seattle School Board. She was the one who sponsored the rule that kids needed permanent addresses to attend specific schools. She said that it was so the "poor homeless youth" wouldn't get lost in the shuffle, but the truth was that she didn't want homeless kids in class with any of her three precious children. Dira walked like her mom, talked like her mom. She wore khaki pants, a white polo shirt, and a blue jacket with a gold emblem on the chest pocket almost every day. I think it was Dira's version of an uppity private-school uniform, even though she was in the fourth grade at Olympic View Elementary, the public school up the street. She looked like a junior real-estate agent and miniversion of her mom. It was creepy.

We were two houses away from Lily's. I looked at my watch. "Oh, man. If I run now, I can catch the next bus downtown to meet my mom and hang out at the bookstore," I said to Lily.

"Okay. Call me when you get back up here to your house," Lily said. She was using her acting abilities to project her voice so it reached Dira's precious ears. "Maybe I can come over to your house after dinner," she added.

"Great. Gotta go. See you, Dira." I sprinted back to Eightieth Street just as the Metro bus pulled up. Once again, perfect timing. I jumped on and swiped my Metro pass through the ticket machine.

It wasn't until I sat down that I realized I was on the wrong bus.

It's not a total disaster to be on the wrong bus. Like I said, I have schedules and routes memorized for sixteen different buses around Seattle. But it's kind of a hassle to have to get off and transfer to another bus. Sometimes it even takes two transfers to get back on the right track.

Turns out I'd jumped onto the 67 instead of the 66. The last stop for the 67 is in the University district, a cool, funky neighborhood by the University of Washington, less than five miles north of downtown.

I got off on "The Ave," the main street running north-south in the U-district, and headed toward my next bus stop.

A cyclist whizzed past me on the sidewalk, almost knocking me out. I saw a flash of the distinctive black-and-purple jersey from Swifty's Bicycle Messengers.

The number 48 bus pulled up, but I resisted the urge to get on it, since it would be the wrong bus yet again. It pulled out, and the view across the street opened up just as two women were putting a sign in the window of the Martin Lee Gallery. I read FEATURING NEW WORK BY MIMI HA . . . The end of the sign had flopped over, so I couldn't see the end of the name. But it doesn't take a spry young detective to figure out what it said.

The number 72 pulled up, rescuing me from the urge to check out the newest Mimi Hansen exhibit.

CHAPTER 14

I WAS IN THAT WEIRD ZONING THING THAT HAPPENS WHEN YOU'RE ON A bus. You know what I mean? I was staring out the window, but I wasn't really seeing anything. I was thinking about Mimi Hansen's paintings, but I wasn't really thinking.

The bus stopped in front of a small art gallery on Eastlake Avenue. The name painted on the window read HENNINGS BOVENG GALLERY. I looked through the glass, and my eyes started to glaze over as all the paintings blurred together. Then one caught my attention.

I snapped out of my trance. I pulled the cord to tell the bus driver I wanted off at the next stop.

I said a hurried thanks to the driver, jumped down two steps, and raced two blocks back to the gallery, where I'd seen a glimpse of a most interesting painting. In fact, you might say that the painting had an interesting "play of light." Just like one that James had been working on at Studio 4.

"May I help you with something?" A man in a black turtleneck and black pants practically jumped on me as I entered the doorway of the gallery. All of Seattle was going crazy with spring fever, and this guy was wearing black from head to toe. Maybe it was a required uniform if you worked in an art gallery.

"I just wanted to look more closely at that blue painting over there," I said. "I think a friend of mine did it."

Mr. Snotty Art Guy looked at me in disbelief.

"Well, James isn't really a good friend of mine or anything. He's a friend of a friend," I said.

"James?" Mr. Snotty Art Guy's voice went up about half an octave, and he swallowed hard.

"James shares a studio space with my friend Nina," I said rather importantly. "I was there yesterday."

Mr. Snotty Art Guy walked back to the desk and started moving papers around. "I don't know this James you mention, but you are welcome to look more closely at the painting as long as you don't touch it," he said, his voice a bit too loud for the small gallery. "Although I doubt you are in a buying mood this afternoon, are you?" he added with a bit of a sneer.

I stood up straight and flipped my hair back over my shoulder. Who was this guy to question my buying ability? Had this guy missed the memo telling him that teens hold important buying power and are the hot, in-demand consumers in the United States? Besides, what if I were as rich as Jordan Walsh, and I could actually buy a painting?

I wanted to tell this guy a thing or two, but the blues in the painting seemed to be calling me to it, inviting me to spend some time looking at it, just like when I'd first seen it downtown at Nina's studio. I couldn't stop looking at it. I stood in front of the painting, twirling a chunk of my hair, a habit I can't seem to shake. It means I'm thinking, but people always misinterpret it as a sign of nervousness. This time I was totally lost in thought. Lost in the painting.

"It's gorgeous! It looks even better out of the studio," I finally said. "You know," I added in a haughty whisper, "I was in the studio when this was created. Aren't there two others in the series?"

"Yes, there are," said Mr. Snotty Art Guy, an eyebrow arching up as he looked me up and down. I could tell I had his attention.

"Do you have the other two? I'd like to see them."
Hey, I had every right to look at art, didn't I?

"Yes, miss, right this way," he said with mock humility. "Please feast your eyes on the *Seattle Streetscapes* series."

He showed me the other two paintings.

"Oh yes! Magnificent! Truly magnificent," I said, trying to act like I was some rich art-collector person. "Hmm . . . That's rather odd, isn't it?"

"What now?" Mr. Snotty Art Guy wasn't playing along with me. He sounded bored.

"There's no signature on these paintings," I replied.

"Surely you know all about that, since you seem to think you're a close personal friend of the artist," he said with a sneer.

"I told you, he's a friend of a friend. James told me he wasn't ready to sign them," I said, resorting to my ordinary Hannah West voice.

"Who's James? Not that I really care," he said.

"Who's James?" I echoed back. Was this guy a nimrod or what? "James . . ." I realized I didn't know his last name. "You know. *James*. The artist."

"James might be an artist, but I assure you that these three paintings are Mimi Hansen originals."

"What?" I gasped.

"Surely an art aficionado like you can recognize a Hansen when you have the rare opportunity to see one," he said.

"Yesterday I was in Nina and James's studio and these paintings were there," I said.

"Perhaps this person you call James was holding the paintings for Mimi Hansen," he said.

"It didn't seem like it. He'd just finished them," I said.

"Perhaps this James was working on some imitation of the brilliant Mimi Hansen's work. Perhaps someone of your age cannot tell a fake when she sees it."

Mr. Snotty Art Guy was getting snottier by the minute. I cleared my throat.

"Could you please tell me why Mimi Hansen didn't sign these paintings?" I asked.

"She will sign these paintings after they are sold at the Honcho auction this weekend," he replied.

"Just like Dorothy Powers's painting?" I asked.

"And I suppose you know Dorothy Powers, too?" he asked.

I don't think he really wanted an answer. I thanked him for his time and kindness to a young girl interested in art. (I can be snotty, too, Mr. Snotty Art Guy.)

I walked out of the gallery and SMASH! I rammed right into someone.

"Gosh, I'm sorry," I stammered.

"Watch where you're going," snapped a female voice. A vaguely familiar female voice. Jordan Walsh's voice. Our eyes connected, and I could tell it took her another second to register who she'd collided with.

"Hey, Jordan," I said, trying my best to be genuinely friendly. "Do you live around here or something?"

"No!" she said, as if I'd insulted her. "I live on Capitol Hill now," she added, a bit more civilly.

"I'd better get going," I said. "I live downtown. In Belltown Towers," I added, trying to one up her.

I saw a flash in Jordan's eyes, but I had no idea what she was thinking.

"See you at school," she said, still avoiding eye contact.

"You must be feeling better," I said, wondering once again why I didn't stop talking and say good-bye because I had a bus to catch, which I did.

"What? No. I mean, yes. I mean, I didn't feel all that great today, but I'm getting better." I might not know Jordan Walsh very well, but I could tell that this girl was clearly uneasy. And she hadn't been sick. She was even blushing as she tried to fabricate a story. Lily always says I have an advantage because my olive-tone skin can hide embarrassment, or at least the blushing that comes with it, better than lots of other people. Jordan had a light golden tan, but the blushing still came through. A taxi driver waiting at the curb honked a horn. Jordan's blush turned scarlet.

"There's my taxi," she said.

Taxi? What sixth grader took a taxi? Oh, wait. Maybe a sixth-grade golden girl who just moved from the suburbs. I might not blush easily, but my face is like an open book. I'm sure Jordan could see what I was thinking. "It's no big deal," she said. "The taxi, that is. My dad insists on it, even though it's only about a mile to my mom's house." I nodded, like I understood completely about overprotective dads who called taxis to take their daughters twenty blocks.

Jordan got in the backseat of the yellow cab. I started walking toward the next bus stop, making sure I was looking straight ahead when the taxi passed me so we could both avoid any awkward waving moments.

Swoosh!

"What the . . ." I cried out, flattening myself against a bakery window. Three other pedestrians were nearly knocked over, too. "Bikes belong in the street!" one guy yelled out.

Yep. You guessed it. A bike on the sidewalk. A bike

powered by a Swifty's bike messenger. The same guy I'd seen on the bus and at the Stimson Building, outside Nina's studio.

I hopped on the next 72 bus heading downtown. I was supposed to meet Mom at the bookstore. I pulled out my sketch pad and turned to the drawing of the bike messenger.

I got an uneasy feeling about this guy even when I was only looking at him in 2–D.

CHAPTER 15

MOM WAVED HELLO BUT SHE WAS TALKING ON HER CELL PHONE WHEN I walked into M Coy Books. She fills in at this cool bookstore by the Pike Place Market when Michael and Michael, the owners, need extra help. I looked through a copy of *Bad Cat* near the cash register until she got off the phone.

"That was Mary Perez," Mom said. "We were going to meet for a quick walk tonight, but she's on a story. She's at the Martin Lee Gallery in the U-district—and another Mimi Hansen was just stolen!"

"I hate the way people say that!" I exclaimed, completely glossing over the fact that Mom had said that another painting had been stolen.

"What?" Mom said.

"You know, they say 'a Mimi Hansen' instead of saying 'a painting.' Like, 'a Mimi Hansen was stolen.' You just said it that way. It drives me crazy," I ranted.

"Somehow I don't think that's what's really bothering you," Mom said.

"I'm just so sick of Mimi Hansen. A week ago I'd never even heard her name. Now I hear it all the time," I said.

A customer walked up to the counter. Mom gave me the "I'll talk to you later" signal.

It took me this long to register exactly what Mom had said. A painting by Mimi Hansen had been stolen in the University district, where I'd just been. In fact, the Martin Lee Gallery was right across the street from where I'd transferred to the southbound bus.

I headed to the back where one of the Michaels was working behind the coffee bar. I sat down on a tall stool and he slid a Thomas Kemper Vanilla Crème Soda down the counter to me. I like sitting at the counter. It feels so grown up, like I'm a regular at a diner.

"Rough day, I take it?" Michael asked.

"Nah. Just an ordinary day in the life of a Seattle middle schooler on the go. I've taken four different buses to get here, and I'm still not home. Not that I even have a home. On top of that, a snotty art guy was extra-special snotty to me because I'm a kid," I whined.

Michael handed me an Uncle Seth cookie. It was one of those huge round shortbread cookies with an inch of fluffy pink frosting on top. "Mmmm . . . sugar bomb," I said, à la Homer Simpson. I gratefully bit into the cookie.

"What's the Honcho auction?" I asked Michael.

"Do you mean Humans of Northwest Cultural and Harmony Organizations?" he asked.

"Huh?" I was paying attention, but this pink frosting was divine.

"It's what Honcho stands for. It started off as a joke, making fun of the Poncho auction, where the super-wealthy people buy things they don't need for outlandish prices, and it all supports the arts," he said.

"Poncho? What a dorky name for an auction," I said.

"It's an acronym, too. Patrons of Northwest Charitable something-or-other Organizations, or something like that," Michael said.

"So why do they need a Honcho auction if there was already a Poncho auction?" I asked between cookie bites.

"A bunch of MegaComp millionaires started Honcho to raise money for the fringe theater groups and undiscovered arts organizations that they thought were overlooked by Poncho. Now the Honcho auction is the biggest arts fund-raiser in the city."

"Who goes?" I asked.

"Anyone can go, as long as you guarantee that you'll spend at least two thousand dollars while you're there," he said.

"Yikes!" I exclaimed.

"Two thousand is just a drop in the bucket," Michael said. "Last year, a puppy was auctioned off for eight thousand dollars."

"For a puppy? What kind of wonder dog was it?"

"A Cavalier King Charles spaniel," Michael said.

"Those are pretty cute dogs," I said. In addition to knowing Metro bus schedules, I've also memorized *The Legacy of the Dog*, a dog-breed book that I used to look at every time I went to M Coy Books. "Still, that's a whole lot of money."

"They're predicting that some of those Mimi Hansen paintings will go for five to twenty thousand dollars apiece," said Michael. "All the recent publicity hasn't hurt, either."

Just then, another customer came and sat at the coffee bar. What are people in Seattle doing drinking coffee at six o'clock in the evening? Obviously this woman needed a double-tall nonfat latte to have the energy to get her home.

Mom came down the steps toward the coffee counter.

"I was listening to KUOW, and I heard about another Mimi Hansen painting being stolen," she said.

"The one from the U-district?" I asked.

"No. Another one. Just in the last few minutes. This last robbery was from a gallery on Eastlake."

CHAPTER 16

MOM AND I WERE BACK AT BELLTOWN TOWERS BY 6:25 P.M. DOROTHY Powers left a message inviting us up for mu shu pork. By 6:28, we were at her door. By 6:29, Mom had told her about the robberies, giving us a full minute to gather in front of the tiny TV in Dorothy's kitchen for the 6:30 news.

Mom's friend Mary was on camera in front of the art gallery where I'd just encountered Mr. Snotty Art Guy. That's right. The same gallery where I'd been less than an hour and a half ago.

"We reported earlier on the theft of a painting by Seattle artist Mimi Hansen. The painting was stolen from the Martin Lee Gallery of Local Art in the University district. Just one hour later, a second painting by artist Mimi Hansen was stolen from yet another gallery. This time the thief struck here, at the Hennings Boveng Gallery on Eastlake," Mary said. The camera backed up to show the storefront of the gallery. Then it zoomed in on Mary again.

"Seattle police are puzzled about who could sneak so swiftly into a gallery during daylight hours, boldly take a piece of artwork off the wall, and disappear without anyone noticing. Traffic was at a standstill on Eastlake Avenue when the theft occurred at the Hennings Boveng Gallery, making it nearly impossible for a getaway car to be involved. Police add that they have no leads on the case, but they have set up a special toll-free hotline for anyone who may have information on the art thefts throughout the city." An 800-number flashed on the screen.

"Hansen has taken the local art world by storm in the last few months. She is known for the wide range of her work. Many call her a prolific artist."

I glanced at Mom and saw her smirk.

"I have artist Mimi Hansen here with me now," Mary continued on TV. "Mimi, tell us a bit about your thoughts about these crimes. Why do you think someone would target your work?"

I was betting that Mary wasn't happy about having to turn over the microphone to Mimi again. Last time Mimi had grabbed the microphone out of Mary's hands and taken over the interview.

This time Mimi kept her hands off the microphone,

but she clearly had a command over the camera. The camera got closer and closer as she talked.

"This is such a cruel, cruel crime," Mimi said. She took off her sunglasses and dabbed a tissue at her eyes. "Art is a precious creative statement that has the ability to reach the soul of every person. Even if they don't understand the complexity of my art, it still resonates with them on some emotional level."

Geesh. Was she being insulting or what?

"I find it hard to believe that a common criminal would have the intellectual ability to appreciate fine art like mine. I think this thief must be a cut above the rest. Obviously I am a rising star, and my art will be worth more and more every year," she continued.

"It will be worth even more now with all this publicity," Mom muttered.

"I can only hope these paintings are returned soon. Some of my work will be featured at the Honcho auction next weekend. In fact, I think it's fair to say that the Mimi Hansen paintings are the most important items at this year's auction. If you are the thief and you are watching now, I beg you to return them. Do it for the arts. Do it for Honcho," Mimi said. She put her sunglasses back on and choked back a sob.

The camera turned back to Mary. "This is Mary

Perez, live on Eastlake Avenue, reporting on the most recent art theft. Back to you, Kathy."

"Oh dear," said Dorothy. She clicked off the TV. "Mimi is such a powerful artist. I hope all this publicity doesn't destroy her or weaken her artistic vision."

I remembered what Michael had said earlier.

"I think she might like all the publicity," I said. Dorothy gave me a surprised, almost dismayed look.

"She does seem to do well when all the cameras are on her, Dorothy," Mom said softly.

"Surely you don't think Mimi had anything to do with this?" Dorothy asked.

Mom and I looked at each other.

"I don't think Mimi is behind the thefts," I started to say. "I think—"

"I agree with you, Hannah," Mom said, pointedly interrupting me. "Mimi isn't stealing them. She certainly couldn't make a quick getaway with those high-heeled shoes she wears." I laughed a little. Mom realized she might have been too glib, so she quickly turned more serious. "I'm sorry. That just slipped out," she said to Dorothy. "But she does seem quite comfortable in front of a camera."

"Mimi seems to magically appear whenever there's a theft—and a TV camera," I said.

"Dear, I think that's a bit of an exaggeration," Dorothy said.

"Maybe I am exaggerating," I admitted. "Do you think Mimi used to work on TV? She seems totally into this camera thing. I don't mean that as an insult or anything," I quickly added.

Neither Mom nor Dorothy had any idea about Mimi's past. It's like six months ago an artist named Mimi Hansen didn't exist. Now she was the talk of the town as well as the toast of the town. I wonder if that was how it worked. You had to get people talking about you before you could be highly regarded for something, for anything.

We thanked Dorothy for dinner. Then Mom headed back down to Owen's apartment, and I took Ruff downstairs for a quick walk around the block. We'd just started down the street when a guy on a bike swerved wide on the sidewalk to miss us, then jumped off his bike while it was still moving, in a graceful style I now expected from bike messengers. This bike guy leaned his bike against a large blue-glazed planter near the Belltown Towers entrance. He straightened his messenger bag and a second bag that was like an artist's portfolio case. He buzzed a number on the intercom security system.

"Yes?" a voice crackled over the intercom.

"Delivery for you, Mr. Chomsky."

Bzzzzzzz.

The front door unlocked, and the same Swifty's bike messenger I'd seen at least two times before headed into the Belltown Towers. After hours. At least an hour after the last delivery time listed on Swifty's Web site. I know that because I checked. No weekend deliveries. No evening deliveries.

Except to Belltown Towers?

CHAPTER 17

I TOOK RUFF FOR A QUICK LOOP AROUND THE BLOCK. I WENT BACK UP TO thirteen and was just getting off the elevator when the door to PH–2 quickly closed. It hadn't been open far. It was as if Mr. Chomsky was checking out the action, seeing who was getting off the elevator. That gave me an idea.

I knocked softly on Mr. Chomsky's door. I stood back from the door and directly in line with the peephole so he could see me. I had a hunch he'd probably been looking through it the entire time anyway.

"Yes?" I heard his voice from the other side of the door.

"Mr. Chomsky? I'm a friend of Dorothy's? Your neighbor across the hall?" Yee gads. My voice was going up at the end of each sentence, like I was asking questions. Time to change to a more assertive tone. "My name is Hannah. I'm her dog walker. I was wondering if I could ask you something."

The door opened a crack. "Something about what? Please be more specific when making an information request," he said.

"Well, I wanted to ask you about delivery services," I said. "I'm working on a social-studies project on different service professions, and I thought I'd see if you ever used UPS, FedEx, or any other kind of services for deliveries . . . maybe even bike messengers?" I hoped I'd been smooth and subtle.

The door opened. "I don't often get visitors," he said. "I'll leave the door open, and we can talk right here." He didn't say that in a cranky way like someone might if they didn't want to invite you inside. Quite the opposite. I think he had impeccable manners, as he must have recognized that my mom would go absolutely ballistic if her daughter went into a stranger's apartment.

And what an apartment! Even from the doorway I could tell it was the mirror image of Dorothy's, but while Dorothy's was full of old-world charm and art and cozy rugs and overstuffed chairs, Mr. Chomsky's apartment was supertechy mixed with the decor of an overcrowded library. Books covered almost every inch of his walls, as well as every flat surface available, including the floor, where more books were precariously stacked into two- and three-foot piles. At least a half-dozen easels were scattered throughout the living room, some with paintings in their frames and some with unframed canvases. Even with the overabundance of books, the place seemed clean and organized. There seemed to be order to the chaos.

There was one spot on the wall where a large plasma screen replaced the books. It looked as if the bookcase had been custom-built to allow for the screen's exact dimensions. Apparently the plasma screen was also his computer monitor, because instead of seeing a television show, the screen was full of a word-processing document. He must have noticed I noticed it, because he took a device out of the pocket of his shirt and whispered into it, "Change screen." The screen switched to a crisp photograph of a tulip field.

I'd expected Mr. Chomsky to be one of two ways: a wild-haired Einstein kind of guy in a bathrobe or a stuffy-looking British guy who wears bow ties all the time, even when playing tennis, which of course he would never do because he never left his apartment. Both of my visions of Mr. Chomsky were wrong. He was dressed pretty normal, with Levi's, a bright white cotton turtleneck with the sleeves pushed up to his elbows, and shiny cowboy boots. He had short gray hair and a clean-shaven face.

"This isn't about social studies, is it?" he asked, and he smiled. It was a genuine smile that you could see was sincere because of the way his eyes seemed to be smiling, too. If I'd expected this hermit to be a deranged old man, I was wrong. Ruff seemed at ease here, too, and so far his instincts had been spot on. Still, I stayed in the doorway in case my own assessment was wrong.

"No, it isn't about social studies. Unless you want to talk about the Byzantine Empire, which is what we're studying right now," I admitted.

"Interesting subject, the Byzantine Empire," he said. "But I suspect that something else has piqued your curiosity."

I was pretty curious about why this cowboy-boot-wearing man stayed in his apartment all the time, but I had enough basic manners under my belt to know I couldn't just blurt out questions about that. "Actually, I want to know about bike messengers," I said. "Dorothy said you have messengers deliver stuff to you."

"That I do. Are you looking to supplement your dog-walking business?" he asked.

"Um, no. I'm just wondering. Did you have a messenger deliver something to you this past Sunday?"

"Sunday? No, no, no. I've tried every bike-messenger service in Seattle, and no one seems to want to work on Sundays. Not even on Saturdays. In this town, it's strictly weekdays."

"Even Swifty's bike messengers?" I asked.

"Especially Swifty's," Mr. Chomsky said. "I used them for years, but they cut back their service hours. No deliveries after six P.M. and no deliveries on weekends."

"Interesting," I said, mulling this over, stalling for time like Columbo from that 1970s detective show. "I thought I just saw a Swifty's bike messenger make a delivery here."

"Oh no, my dear. I'm sure you didn't see a messenger coming here after-hours," Mr. Chomsky said with a wink. "Now, if you don't mind, I need to get back to my research. If you decide you want to discuss the Byzantine Empire, please come back. It's not my primary research focus these days, but I did devote a few years during the 1950s to it," he said. His manner, although still friendly, turned abrupt.

"Research?" I must have looked dumbfounded.

"Yes. I need to get back to my research," he said again.

"Well, thank you," I said, bending down to scoop up Ruff. It was an artful ploy to give me a chance to stall and look one last time inside his apartment.

"Aaahhhh . . ." I started to gasp. "I mean, aaaah-choooo . . ." I faked a sneeze.

I'd just seen two large, flat packages wrapped in plain brown paper leaning against Mr. Chomsky's worktable, right alongside a country landscape with the name Mimi Hansen scrawled in the lower right corner.

CHAPTER 18

AS SOON AS I GOT HOME, I CALLED LILY TO DISCUSS THIS LATEST development in the case. It was pretty clear that Mr. Chomsky was hiding something with his off-hours messenger deliveries. And what was with those wrapped-up paintings? Did he have something to do with the thefts?

"And why do I keep seeing the same bike messenger all the time?" I asked Lily.

"Twice? You've seen this guy twice, and you call that *all the time*?" she asked.

"I think it's been three times. And I think it's significant. Three is always significant. Like that blue painting I saw in Nina's studio. The one that I thought James painted, but the rest of the world says Mimi Hansen painted. I've seen that same painting three times now. Three times! That's significant."

"I'd say *weird* would be a better word choice than *significant*," Lily said.

"It's even weirder that it's a Mimi Hansen painting," I said. "Something isn't quite right. It really seemed like it was part of James's work at the studio. And why do I keep seeing bike messengers?"

"Do you know how many messenger companies there are in Seattle?" Lily asked.

"No, but I think you're about to tell me."

"That's right. I am. There are eleven. And Swifty's isn't even the biggest, according to my dad."

"And all of this supports the total significance of me seeing Swifty's bike messengers repeatedly," I said.

"Maybe you notice them more because they wear purple. You've had this thing for purple ever since we were in second grade."

She had me there.

"We need to get back on track with our case," I said.

"It's not like you've been hired to solve this or something," Lily said, as if that somehow needed clarifying.

"That's what makes us the perfect sleuths. No one notices teen girls."

"We're sleuths? We're teens?"

"Yes, we're sleuths. And we're almost teens."

"Cool. Let's look at this James guy. Maybe Mimi is working on some top-secret project with him at that studio," Lily said.

"Nina can't keep a secret. I think if Mimi Hansen were working in her studio, she'd spill the beans. She definitely would have told Mom. And Mom would have said something to me," I said.

"Parents can keep secrets, you know," Lily said.

"Some parents can keep secrets. But Maggie West can't," I countered.

"Okay. Let's say that Mimi wasn't using that studio. Maybe James saw Mimi's work and was copying it," Lily said.

"But Mimi stopped by the studio yesterday," I said. "If James is imitating her work, he's totally busted."

"That brings us back to the theory that she uses the Studio 4 space to paint."

Lily's theory that Mimi painted in the same space as Nina wasn't exactly taking hold of my imagination. But *Frankenstein* was. I stayed up late reading for my English quiz the next day. I have to admit that I thought Frankenstein was a zombie guy with bolts in his neck. And even though I'd heard people refer to it as "Frankenstein's monster," in the original story the monster is nameless.

Sort of like Mimi Hansen paintings. They might have titles, but they're nameless. Or signatureless.

CHAPTER 19

THE 6:30 DISCO ALARM CAME WAY TOO EARLY FRIDAY MORNING. I woke up expecting to be a character in some gothic novel. But then I looked out Owen Henderson's window at the Bainbridge Island ferryboat crossing Elliott Bay, and I snapped back to the twenty-first-century reality.

I didn't give Mimi Hansen a second thought. Heck, I hadn't even thought about Jordan Walsh. But then I got to Chavez Middle School. That's when I saw Mimi Hansen's little white convertible zip past me and park in the bus zone. And get this: A Channel 4 News camera was pointed right at her when she pulled up.

The camera person came closer to the car. Mimi hopped out and smoothed her skirt. Jordan got out on her side, tossing her backpack over her shoulder and putting on sunglasses.

The vice principal gets a little testy whenever

someone parks in the bus-loading zone. But I hardly think it's newsworthy. Something was definitely up.

"You're never going to guess who's here," I said to Lily. We met at our regular spot, the spindly maple tree at the Fifth Avenue side of Chavez Middle.

"Let me guess. Channel 4 News?" Lily said.

"Well, yeah, them, too. But that isn't who I'm talking about. Mimi's here."

Lily didn't seem to connect right away.

"Mimi Hansen is at school. And so is a news crew."

"What's up with that?" Lily asked.

"I think we're about to find out," I said. Grace Malone, the mouth of the middle school, headed straight for us.

"What's up, Grace?" I asked.

"You'll never guess why Channel 4 is here!" Grace oozed with excitement.

"Are they here to give you the Perkiest Student Award?" I asked. When Grace giggled, I kind of hated myself for being sarcastic to her.

"You know about all those paintings by that famous artist that have been stolen?" Grace whispered.

We nodded encouragingly.

"Well, it turns out that Jordan Walsh is her daughter!

Channel 4 is doing one of those human-interest thingies, you know, where they follow people around to show how famous people are really ordinary and all that. So they're getting some shots of Mimi and Jordan at school," said Grace. "I bet I can guess the angle they'll take. It will be all about how Jordan is a budding genius artist, too. This is soooo exciting!"

Lily and I rolled our eyes at each other. I could tell that Grace was thinking over what kind of things she could say on camera, just in case the Channel 4 News crew decided to interview one of Jordan's classmates.

I'm not a TV expert or anything, but I'm pretty sure that following a middle-school student's mother around Chavez Middle wasn't going to be a ratings hit. The crew was probably just getting a few shots of Mimi letting her daughter off at school, and that was it.

Boy, was I wrong.

"Oh, brother," I murmured. A camera was aimed right at each of us as we entered the art studio.

Jack Finster made a face into the camera. Demi Demick gave a peace sign. And I, Hannah West, looked at my shoes and walked into the classroom as quickly as possible. I'm sure we all made fascinating TV.

A woman wearing a red suit jacket and tons of makeup was talking to Ms. Murdoch at the front of the room. Ms. Murdoch was smiling and nodding, but she looked a little tense. Maybe she was worried that she'd end up on TV or something.

"Class, we have a reporter here from Channel 4 News today," Ms. Murdoch said. That explained why the red-jacket woman was wearing so much makeup. "They're doing a story on Jordan's mother, Mimi Hansen, and how she volunteers to help at Chavez Middle School's arts programs."

Huh? Mimi Hansen volunteered at school? This was Jordan's first week at this school. Besides, Mimi didn't seem like a PTA mom or the kind of mom who helped out in the classroom. Especially not in middle school, when no self-respecting student would allow a parent inside the school. But there she was, wearing a big blue work shirt with the sleeves all rolled up, like she was ready to finger-paint with us or something.

Ms. Murdoch told us we'd be sketching a still life that Mimi had arranged for us. She aimed some lights at the worktable, lighting up a Buddha, a pyramid, and a tall vase with spiky branches coming out.

"Try walking around the room and looking at this from all angles," Mimi called to us, but she was really talking into the camera.

The camerawoman followed Jordan as she slowly circled the room. Each time she stopped, the camerawoman zoomed over to the still life, as if trying to see what Jordan might be seeing.

"You know, I just don't get into the classroom as much as I'd like," Mimi Hansen said to the reporter.

"How often do you help in your daughter's school?" the reporter asked.

"Try 'never,'" I heard someone say. Could it be? Yes! Those words of truth came from Jordan Walsh herself. I'd assumed that Jordan was totally digging this TV thing. But she actually looked mortified.

"What was that?" the reporter asked, looking around the room.

"I said, 'not often enough,'" Mimi said through a clenched-teeth smile.

"Jordan, as you know, your mom won't allow us into her private studio at your home. Can you tell us what it's like to work on art projects side by side at your home studio?" the reporter asked with a blindingly white smile.

"Actually, Mom doesn't—" Jordan began.

Mimi rushed over to Jordan's side. "We really like to keep our home life private, don't we, honey?" Mimi said. I think she meant Jordan when she said "honey," but she was talking directly to the reporter.

I was paying way too much attention to all this. I tried concentrating on Buddha.

Suddenly the room got darker. I looked up and realized that the TV lights had turned off. Mimi flounced out of the room.

"'Bye, Mom," I heard Jordan call. Mimi turned and gave a dramatic wave. "Good-bye, darling," she said with a smile. But the smile and the wave were aimed at the TV camera, not at her daughter.

I had an icky feeling in my stomach. I wanted to look at Jordan, but I didn't want to. I looked anyway.

She was bent over her sketch pad. But I could tell she was crying.

I couldn't believe it. I actually felt sorry for Jordan Walsh.

CHAPTER 20

JORDAN WASN'T IN SOCIAL STUDIES OR LANGUAGE ARTS. GRACE MALONE told Mr. Ogata it was because she was busy being interviewed for a prime-time TV special.

"Thank you for the update, Grace," Mr. Ogata said. "I'll make a note of that right next to the column where I'm marking her absent."

I was thinking about Jordan so much that when I did finally see her at lunch, I had to say something.

"Hey," I said. I was trying to put a lot of compassion and kindness into that one-word greeting.

"Is it okay if I sit here?" Jordan asked. She was sitting on the stoop where Lily and I usually hang out in the morning and where I like to sit and sketch during lunch. "I mean, I know this is your spot and everything. I just don't feel like being down there." She motioned toward the bed of social activity in the main lunchroom.

"It's cool," I said. "Want a taquito?"

"No, but thanks," Jordan said. "What do you draw when you're sitting here?"

"Just regular stuff," I said. I didn't mention the recent sketch of her as Medusa. "You know, I just have to keep drawing." I glanced at her. "Do you feel like that? Like you have to draw?"

"Um, I don't think I'm actually very artistic," Jordan said.

"You must be, or you wouldn't be in Ms. Murdoch's art class," I said. Geesh. I hadn't known I could be so polite and supportive.

"Ms. Murdoch asked to have me in her class. I have no idea why."

"Maybe she thinks you're genetically programmed to be an artist," I said. "You know, because of your mom and all."

"Pleeeeeze," Jordan said. "Mom wasn't born an artist. She just became one. In fact, when she broke up with my stepdad, she thought all artists were airhead idiots. But maybe that's because my stepdad had an affair with an artist."

"Really?" I said, in what I hoped was an encouraging tone to keep her going. I was part nosy and part sincere.

"Yeah. Mom was all wrapped up in being a hotshot public-relations person. She worked all the time. All she talked about was Wentworth Enterprises. My stepdad was a Wentworth. But he was never at work. He wasn't at home, either. He was having an affair with a twenty-two-year-old art student who won a design competition for the new Wentworth logo. My stepdad got a new logo and a new wife. Mom got a divorce and a washed-up career." Jordan delivered this family history with a monotone voice.

"That's brutal," I said. "Maybe your mom used art to work through her problems, or something."

"If she did, I sure never saw her do it. She was telling that Channel 4 reporter about how private she is about her studio at home. It's so private that I've never even seen it," she said.

"You mean, it's locked and you can't go in?"

"I mean that there isn't even a studio at our house," Jordan said. "Not at our old house in Bellevue and not in our new house here in Seattle."

I had a clear picture of Jordan from her downcast eyes and the way she was talking. She might be a rich kid from the suburbs, but she was also a shy kid at a new school.

"I have to go now," Jordan said, looking uncomfortable.

"Sure. Later," I said.

• • •

I made it back to the apartment at Belltown Towers after school without witnessing any art crimes. I'd call that a successful day. Mom was sitting at the dining-room table with her laptop computer. She had her back to the window so that she wouldn't be distracted by the view of the water and the ferryboats. I knew that meant she was on a deadline.

"What are you working on?" I asked. I grabbed a Granny Smith apple from the refrigerator.

"Calendar listings for *Art Voice*," she said, without looking up. Once a month she writes a column that gives previews of all the visual-arts shows going on up and down the West Coast. Her column is called "The West View." (Clever title, isn't it? I thought of it.) Mom's column has quite a following.

"This is just unbelievable," she grumbled.

"What's unbelievable?" I asked.

"Seven different galleries have planned Mimi Hansen shows this summer. They all claim that they'll have 'new, never-before-viewed' pieces by her," Mom said, shaking her head in bewilderment. "It just doesn't seem possible that one person could create so much."

"Or be so *prolific*?" I asked.

"She's prolific, all right," Mom said. "The mind-boggling part is, so far, what I've seen, her stuff is actually good. It's so varied. It's like she's twenty different artists all at once."

"Interesting," I said. "Maybe she has multiple personalities and each one paints differently." Interesting, indeed.

"That could be one explanation, if this were a made-for-TV movie or something," Mom said. "The only thing I can think of is that maybe she was secretly working for years and years, and she just didn't show anyone her work."

"I don't think so," I said. "My multiple-personality theory would seem more likely after what I learned today."

I told Mom about what Jordan told me at lunch.

"Wow. That's a heavy load for a kid," Mom said. She got up to get a cup of tea. I sat down at her laptop and Googled *Mimi Hansen*, *Wentworth Enterprises*, and *Walsh*.

"Even if she doesn't have multiple personalities, it looks like she's had multiple names," I said. "Did you ever hear of Mimi Wentworth? She used to be married to some guy named Wentworth. There's a whole bunch of articles here about Mimi Walsh Wentworth and the Mills Brothers campaign."

"I remember reading about Mimi Wentworth! She was a PR person for Mills Brothers, a business that landed a bunch of high-power executives in jail," Mom said. "A lot of MegaComp millionaires invested their money in Mills Brothers, which was supposed to be a company to rival both Starbucks and Amazon. I don't remember the details, just that it was a big fat fraud. Mimi Wentworth got people to invest money in nothing."

"But nothing happened to Mimi Wentworth?" I asked.

"She just sort of dropped out of sight," Mom said.

"Until now," I said. I showed Mom the computer screen. I'd placed a photo of Mimi Wentworth, the marketing genius, next to Mimi Hansen, the artist. I hadn't been able to find a photo of Mimi Hansen without her sunglasses, though.

They looked like two completely different people. Mimi Wentworth had big hair. Really big hair. She had big lips, too. But mostly she had lots and lots of makeup on.

"Now watch this," I said.

I went into Photoshop and took the photo of Mimi Wentworth. I changed her long auburn curly hair to a chin-length straight blond style. I made her lips smaller and a lighter color. I toned down her makeup.

"Getting closer . . ." Mom said.

Then I put dark sunglasses on her to cover her blue eyes.

"Bingo!" Mom said.

CHAPTER 21

NOW I KNEW THAT MIMI HANSEN USED TO BE MIMI WENTWORTH. So what, right? I knew it meant something. I just wasn't sure what.

The big Mimi question remained: How in the world did Mimi Hansen create so many paintings so quickly?

I headed up the fire stairs to the penthouse floor to pick up Ruff. I opened the door to the thirteenth floor just as someone with a Swifty's-bike-messenger jersey disappeared behind the elevator's closing doors.

"Dorothy!" I ran to the door of Dorothy Powers's apartment and rang the doorbell.

"Come in if you're Hannah," she called.

"I don't think that's the safest way to answer the door," I said as I walked into her apartment. "Is everything okay in here? Did you just get something delivered?"

"I'm fine, dear. But nothing was delivered," Dorothy

called from the couch. She had her right leg propped up over the side of the couch. I knew she was having knee trouble and that she tried to elevate her leg as much as possible.

"I just saw a bike messenger in the hall get on the elevator."

"There must have been a delivery to Marvin Chomsky across the hall. He has messengers deliver everything to him, even toilet paper," Dorothy said. "But mostly his deliveries are for his research and his groceries."

"Just what exactly does Mr. Chomsky research?" I asked.

"He's an art historian. Quite famous in his field, I believe," Dorothy said. "Apparently he's in great demand all over the world."

"But he never leaves his apartment?" I asked.

"Not that I know of," Dorothy said. "He's mentioned museums from Oslo and Amsterdam that send him paintings to research since he won't travel to them."

"He doesn't even come across the hall?" I asked.

"He's turned down all my offers to come over for coffee."

"Maybe he's holding out for a dessert invitation," I said.

"Maybe he is." Dorothy chuckled.

"Ready for your walk, boy?" I asked the little terrier. Ruff ran to the kitchen and got his leash. I'd trained him to do that in just two sessions. "Such a good boy," I said, rewarding him with a dried-liver treat.

"I'll see you later, Dorothy," I called as Ruff tugged at his leash. "Keep your knee propped up. I'll get Ruff tuckered out for you."

Ruff loves to walk, and he's pretty fast for a little guy. But the vet had said he was a few pounds overweight. I was under strict orders not to let people feed him on our walks. This turned out to be the toughest part of the job. Ruff knows almost everyone in the Belltown neighborhood. And almost everyone wants to give him a treat.

We headed south on First Avenue. There are lots of restaurants on First Avenue with outside eating areas, but it was too early for the after-work crowd. Restaurant workers were just setting up the outside tables. It was safe territory for Ruff at 4:30, but in about thirty minutes I'd have to pick a different route if I didn't want him to go crazy wanting bits of bread or food from people's plates.

We stopped at a little park on Second and Bell. It was one of Ruff's favorite sniffing areas. There were always people and dogs at the park. Ruff sniffed his hello to seven dogs. We were just leaving the park when a cyclist on the sidewalk cruised past us, almost mowing down Ruff.

"Use the street!" I screamed. Geesh. Another cyclist cut around a corner sharply. Ruff jumped back and yelped.

"Come on! You guys aren't supposed to be on the sidewalk!" I yelled.

I started yelling before I really looked at who was pedaling. I saw the familiar purple and black. A Swifty's bicycle messenger. The rider turned around and glared at me, and then he zipped around the corner. The same guy I'd seen three times before. It figures.

"If a crime happens right here, right now, it's definitely not a coincidence," I muttered to Ruff. I looked around and listened, as if waiting for a frenzy of activity and the wail of sirens. Nothing.

Ruff and I were right by Wired Café. I looked through the window, but there was a glare from the sun, and I couldn't really see who was inside. I could tell there were some people in line for coffee. I peeked through the doorway and saw Nina working behind the espresso counter. She looked up and waved me in. I pointed down to Ruff. I couldn't go inside with a dog. Nina held up three fingers. That meant to hang on for three minutes and she'd come outside. I signaled back "okay" with three fingers up.

Wired keeps a bowl of dog water outside, and Ruff eagerly lapped some up.

"We'll need to have everything ready for Mimi to review later tonight at The Factory." A voice traveled outside through the open door. The voice sounded vaguely familiar, but I couldn't place it.

"She wasn't at all happy when she stopped by the studio earlier this week," said a man with a Jamaican accent.

"I just don't know how much longer we can keep working at this pace," the first voice said.

Two people came outside, each clutching a Wired Café cup. Ms. Murdoch, my art teacher, stopped when she saw me.

"Hannah! What fun to see you outside of school!" she said. "I'd like you to meet my friend James."

"I believe we met at the studio," James said. "You are a friend of Nina's, right?"

I wanted to blurt out "Yes, I saw you at your studio when you were painting the *Seattle Streetscapes*, which looked suspiciously like a trio of paintings by Mimi Hansen." But I didn't get a chance because Ms. Murdoch put her arm around someone who had just arrived at Wired. Someone in a purple-and-black Swifty's jersey. "And this is my brother, Conner," Ms. Murdoch said.

Her brother held out his hand. "Conner Murdoch. I think we've run into each other around town," he said. "Or at least I almost ran into you a couple of times."

Conner Murdoch was the same cyclist who'd almost just plowed over Ruff. The same one I'd seen outside the Hennings Boveng Gallery. The same one I'd seen in the background of the news and in front of my building the other night. The same one I'd drawn in my sketch pad on Monday.

Was he the same one I'd seen outside Belltown Towers the day we'd moved in?

CHAPTER 22

NINA CAME OUT WITH A MEXICAN HOT CHOCOLATE FOR ME. IT DOESN'T matter how hot or how cold it is, I am a sucker for this concoction of semisweet chocolate, cinnamon, vanilla bean, and cream. It's nothing like the instant hot cocoa with dehydrated minimarshmallows we have at home. Nina says she makes it special for me because she's part Mexican, but it's actually a regular drink on the Wired menu. She brought a big dog-cookie dog treat for Ruff. I vowed I'd walk him another ten minutes to make up for veering from his diet.

"Are you guys leaving now?" Nina asked Ms. Murdoch and James. "I'll catch up with you at The Factory tonight. I'll be there for a while before I have to come back here to close Wired."

The three of them left.

"You know my art teacher?" I asked.

"It's a small town if you're an artist," Nina said. "It seems like we all know each other."

"Is her brother an artist?"

"No, but he's into it," Nina said. "I guess he knows Mimi Hansen and lots of gallery folks. I don't really know much about him. He's cute, isn't he?"

"I keep seeing him around. Usually right around the same time that the paintings disappear," I said. "Look, I even sketched him a couple of times."

"Hmm . . . pretty good, Hannah. Maybe you agree with me and you think Conner Murdoch is a hottie." Nina smiled and winked at me.

"Ewwww! He's old, Nina!"

"Not too old for me. Besides, I'm sure it's just a coincidence that you keep seeing him. Swifty's headquarters is just over on Wall Street, so it makes sense you'd see him around here."

"Maybe," I reluctantly agreed. It was time to get back home if I wanted to have dinner with Mom before she left for work at Wired.

When I got into the lobby of Belltown Towers, a large, flat parcel wrapped in brown paper caught my attention. What can I say? I'm like a magnet for these packages these days. And this one was just leaning next to the mailboxes. It was addressed to Mr. Chomsky, with no return address. Time for me to be a Good Samaritan.

I wrestled the three-foot-by-three-foot package onto the elevator and pushed the PH button. I lugged the parcel down the hallway and breathlessly knocked on PH–2.

"Hannah!" Mr. Chomsky said warmly. "Did you decide to come back to discuss Byzantine history?"

"Not yet. I have a package for you," I said. "Don't they usually bring packages up to you?"

"It's different with every service." He sighed.

I decided not to beat around the bush anymore. "So, Mr. Chomsky, what's being delivered to you these days?"

"Usually musty old documents and paintings," he said. "Museums hire me to research the history and authenticity of paintings from all around the world. Lately I've been researching the origins of some local contemporary paintings. It's a case you might be a bit familiar with."

All of my suspicions about Mr. Chomsky being the art thief dissipated. He seemed as authentic as they come. I looked past him into the living room filled with paintings and books. My eyes stopped on the same blue painting I'd seen in his apartment the other night.

"Is that a Mimi Hansen?" I asked. "I mean, is that a painting by Mimi Hansen?" I asked more correctly.

"Ah, a good question, Miss West, no matter how you choose to frame it," Mr. Chomsky laughed at his pun.

"Also, an excellent question no matter how you phrase it. As you may have noticed, there is no signature on this painting. But perhaps the signature would not tell us the truth anyway. It seems that at this point in time, this painting's origins are a bit of a mystery."

As you can tell by now, I love a mystery.

"Surprise!" Lily called when I walked into our apartment.

"Hey, what are you doing here? How'd you get here?" I asked.

"Dad was meeting a friend at the Belltown Pub, so he gave me a ride down here early for our big overnight extravaganza," she said.

"Cool! Mom has to work tonight. We can hang out in Belltown and stay out late!" I said.

"Wait a minute there," Mom said. Her laptop was put away, and she was wearing her Wired uniform. They don't really have uniforms, but Mom has a definite look when she's working at Wired. Tonight it was a pink tie-dyed tank top with one of those long slinky sarong-style skirts that tie. She had on big black Dr. Martens boots, which she insisted on wearing if she was on her feet for a long shift. Her massive blond curly hair was in a ponytail on the top of her head. She has to keep her hair up or she'll start playing with it, twirling it just like I do (she says she's not sure if I got it from her or she got it from me). I watched as she put in her earrings, which takes a while since she has four piercings on one ear and seven on the other.

"I know you're kidding about being out late, but we need to go over some ground rules, girls," she said. "Belltown is crazy on Friday nights. You can come down to Wired if you want to hang out for a while. You'll need to call me to tell me when you're leaving Belltown Towers so I'll know when you'll be at Wired. Then you'll need to get back here before it gets dark. You can stay up as late as you can stand it, as long as you're in pajamas and have your teeth brushed and flossed by ten o'clock."

Nothing like a mother to put you in your place. Even a mother with eleven ear piercings.

Lily's dad had given her thirty dollars to order Chinese food. We were sitting on Owen's balcony looking at the water.

"I could get used to you guys living here," Lily said. "It's so exciting to be downtown. I can pretend we're in New York or something."

"Yes, dahling, 'tis magnificent here," I drawled. I put

on sunglasses and handed a pair of Mom's to Lily. The view from Belltown Towers was truly incredible, but it faced west, and the sun was right in our eyes.

"What kind of action do you see on the street down there?" Lily asked.

"I don't really look down that much," I admitted. "It makes me kind of dizzy. I almost threw up the first day we were here."

Lily stood on the edge of the balcony and peered over. My stomach fluttered just watching her be that close. She was looking straight down at the sidewalk. "Well, you're not missing much down there," she said. "Wait! Isn't that Nina?"

I carefully looked down, my sweaty palms clutching the balcony railing. She's kind of easy to pick out in a crowd, especially when she's wearing her hair loose like it was tonight. Her thick, wavy hair fell past her shoulders. Its near-jet-blackness was a stark contrast to the tight white T-shirt she was wearing.

"It is. I wonder what she's doing here. She knows Mom is working tonight," I said.

But Nina didn't stop at Belltown Towers. She crossed the street and went to the middle of the block. She paused in front of a black door. Then she went inside.

"Do you think she has a hot date?" Lily asked.

I reached for another potsticker. "Believe me, if we were living close to a guy Nina liked, chances are she'd move in here with us. But she hasn't been hanging around much at all. Mom says she's busy with some project."

"Maybe that's her project right down there," Lily said.

A guy was definitely waiting outside the same black door that Nina had just entered. I grabbed the mini-binoculars that Owen kept on top of the bookcase.

"Uh-oh," I said.

"What? Who is it? What's he look like?" Lily grabbed the binoculars from me. "Big deal. It's just a bike messenger from Swifty's." She lowered the binoculars and turned to look at me. "Come on, Hannah. It's probably just a coincidence. This guy probably just has a delivery to make to whatever business is across the street."

"It's after seven on a Friday night," I pointed out.

Lily looked through the binoculars again. "Mr. Bike Messenger is kind of cute. Is this the same guy you've been seeing all around town? You never said anything about him being cute."

"Yes! Will you listen to me? It's the same guy. And get this: He's Ms. Murdoch's brother," I said. "His name is Conner. Nina thinks he's cute, too."

"It looks like maybe Nina does have a hot date," Lily said. She handed the binoculars back to me. Nina had answered the door across the street and was holding it open for Conner Murdoch to go inside.

"Let's go see where they're going," I said.

"Ick. If they're on a date, we can't go spy on them," Lily said.

"But what if they're not on a date? What if he's about to steal a Mimi Hansen painting and Nina's in the wrong place at the wrong time?"

"Highly unlikely."

"Yet you're entertaining the possibility," I countered.

Dog walking is excellent for undercover work. Five minutes later, Lily, Ruff, and I were out the front door of Belltown Towers.

"Oops. Forgot something," I said, and turned right back into the lobby. I dragged Ruff back in after me. Lily followed grudgingly. "What's up?" she started. I put my finger to my lips. "Shhh! Step back so that guy doesn't see us."

It was Mr. Snotty Art Guy from the Hennings Boveng Art Gallery. He was still wearing a black turtleneck, black pants, a black jacket, and even black sunglasses. "Hello. The sun is on its way down. What's with the glasses?" Lily whispered.

"What's with the whispering?" I whispered back. "It's not like he can hear us out there."

Mr. Snotty Art Guy was carrying a big flat artist's portfolio, the kind with the handles on top. He jaywalked across First Avenue.

"He must not be from Seattle," Lily said.

"I was just going to say that!" I said. No one jaywalks in Seattle. Cops on bikes give out tickets like crazy when people try to cross the street without a "Walk" signal. No one crosses in the middle of a downtown street. No one but Mr. Snotty Art Guy, that is.

"He's heading for that same door," I said. "Come on!" I motioned to Lily and Ruff. We headed back out on the sidewalk. Mr. Snotty Art Guy looked like he had just rung the bell across the street. He said something into the intercom. He was pacing in front, smoking a cigarette. The door opened and he headed in.

"Okay. You've convinced me. We have to check this out!" I said. We crossed the street and went up to the black door. The nameplate by it was blank.

"Hannah! What are you doing here? And is that Lily Shannon?"

We turned to see Ms. Murdoch, my art teacher.

CHAPTER 23

"MS. MURDOCH!" I SAID.

"What are you girls doing in Belltown on a Friday night?" she asked.

"Mom and I are . . ." I almost told her about the house-sitting gig we had at Belltown Towers. But Lily grabbed Ruff from me.

"Hannah and I are visiting a friend, Owen, who lives in Belltown Towers across the street," she said.

"Right," I chimed in. "Owen asked us to walk his friend's dog. This is Ruff. Remember, you saw him at Wired this afternoon? He needs to walk a lot."

"What are you up to tonight, Ms. Murdoch?" Lily asked.

"Oh, I'm on my way to a party here," she said. She didn't look like she was going to a party. She was wearing overalls with paint splatters on them, sneakers with rips in them. Her hair was in two braids, and she had a red bandanna tied over the top of her head. "I know. I know. My students never like to think I have a life after school or that I might go to a party," Ms. Murdoch was saying, a bit too enthusiastically if you ask me.

"Well, have fun, then," I said lamely.

"Rock on," Lily added. Even lamer.

"We'll just head on our walk now," I said.

We walked a few steps away and heard Ms. Murdoch whisper something into the intercom. Someone buzzed her in.

"Excuse me, will you?" a haughty voice said. We looked up to see that we'd almost run into Mimi Hansen. Of course, she didn't recognize me. She barely even acknowledged that Lily and I were human beings. We were in her way, and that was inconvenient for her.

"Sorry," we both said meekly. We walked a few more yards down the street and then slyly looked behind us to see Mimi go through that same black door.

"We've got to get into that building," I said emphatically.

"And you've got to take me with you when you get in," said a voice behind us.

I turned to see Jordan Walsh.

"Jordan?" I asked in disbelief. "What are you doing down here?"

"I'm supposed to meet my dad at Mama's Mexican

Kitchen. But he's running late, as usual. So I guess my mom's going to be stuck with me for a while," she said. "She told me she'd be here in case of an emergency, but she wouldn't tell me what was going on. I guess this is an emergency, though, since she can't expect me to hang around downtown for an hour all by myself. I'm going inside to find out what's up."

"Maybe it's just a party," Lily said.

"I don't think so," Jordan said. "She was acting a little too weird for it to be just a party. I have to find out what she's hiding." She started to look a little weepy.

"You've watched them in there before, haven't you?" I asked Jordan.

"Not here," Jordan said. "But yeah, I have watched them. I was never really sure what was going on, though."

"Watched who?" Lily asked.

"The artists?" I asked gently.

She nodded again. "The real artists."

"I thought so," I said. It all made sense to me now.

Someone else was creating the valuable paintings that were being sold as "Mimi Hansens."

"Is this The Factory?" I asked Jordan, remembering the conversation I'd overheard Ms. Murdoch have at Wired Café.

Jordan nodded yet again.

Just then the door opened. All of us instinctively ducked into the doorway of Sticky Fingers Bakery.

Mr. Snotty Art Guy and Conner Murdoch were on the sidewalk. "I didn't know your sister was part of The Factory crew," Mr. Snotty Art Guy said. "I guess Mimi Hansen's got the whole family on the payroll now."

"I didn't know Shelley was working for Mimi, either," Conner said. "It seems like the whole city is."

"I gotta go to Ralph's," Mr. Snotty Art Guy said.

"I'm heading back in," Conner said.

"Leave the door open so I don't have to buzz upstairs again. They're getting cranky up there. I'll be back in five."

"Here's our chance," I whispered. We all moved to the black door.

"Let me go first," Jordan said. We followed her up a flight of stairs. The carpet on the stairs was worn-out, and it seemed like every other stair creaked. We went up another flight of stairs and then down a gloomy hallway lit with a solitary naked lightbulb hanging from the ceiling. We could hear music coming through a doorway at the end of the hall. We also heard footsteps coming up the stairs.

"In here!" I beckoned Lily and Jordan into a small room, and we closed the door. We waited for the footsteps to go past us. Ruff started sniffing around. "Please be quiet, please be quiet," I silently willed Ruff to not make any sudden dog noises. But he just kept sniffing. He nudged Lily over, and his nose went right for a small hole in the wall.

"Ruff! Over here!" I whispered. I pulled a dried-liver treat out of my pocket and lured him over to the corner. Then I got down on all fours and peeked through the hole. It looked right into the big room, but it was way too low to see anything except feet and legs. But two feet higher there was a wide crack that made quite a handy portal into the other room. They were all there: Nina; James; Ms. Murdoch; her brother, Conner; and about six other people. Each person—except Conner Murdoch—was at an easel. To the unsuspecting eye, it might look like some kind of hip art jam, with a bunch of artists hanging out together and making art to loud music. But no one here looked like they were having fun. In fact, they all looked tortured.

I could see why.

Mimi Hansen came into view. She walked by each easel. "Hmm . . . this one might work. And this one works. Very Hansen. Yes, that's good. Very Hansen. Yes, yes. That's so Hansen!" She clapped her hands to get their attention, just like she was a first-grade teacher.

Maybe we could see only part of her through the hole, but her voice was coming through loud and clear.

"Listen up, people. It's only a week until the Honcho auction. I need each of you to finish one more painting by Wednesday. There are only two here tonight that are ready for me to sign," she said. "You really need to crank it up." She walked over to a painting James was doing. "I'm ready to sign this one." She elbowed James out of the way.

"It's not actually finished," he said.

"I say it is finished, and that means it's finished," Mimi hissed. "You need to start another painting. Now!"

"She's so mean. Oops. Sorry!" Lily grimaced toward Jordan.

"It's okay," Jordan whispered back.

Mimi took the painting from James's easel and brought it over to a large worktable. Mr. Snotty Art Guy was back in the room now. He photographed the painting and wrote something down in a ledger.

"Listen up, people!" Mimi called to the room. She turned down the music on the boom box. "You can take a break in ten. But it looks like it will be a long night."

Just then Jordan's cell phone rang. *Oops,* she mouthed. Lily and I glared at her.

"Were you expecting anyone else?" I heard Mimi ask.

Jordan sighed and climbed out of the closet. We peered out the door as she walked down the hall toward the studio and Mimi Hansen.

"Hello, Mother," Jordan said.

"Jordan! What are you doing here? You know I must work in private," Mimi said. That was a hoot, since she certainly wasn't working—and there were nine people who were.

"Don't worry, Mother. I'm not here to bother you. I just need some cash," Jordan said. She held out her hand, palm up, with the air of a bored pampered teenager.

Hmm . . . *Not bad, Jordan,* I thought. Maybe she could join the Lily Shannon Acting Troupe.

"Come on! Let's get out of here!" I carried Ruff and led Lily out of the closet, down the hall, back down two flights of stairs, and out onto First Avenue.

CHAPTER 24

"DO YOU HAVE A PLAN?" LILY ASKED.

"My plan is gadgets. We need some gadgets," I said. Ruff barked. "Thank you for not doing that inside," I added, nuzzling my nose into his neck.

We went up to our apartment and grabbed Mom's digital camera. Mom needed it for her work at the magazine, and she had made it very clear that I was not supposed to touch it. But these were extraordinary circumstances. On second thought, a video camera would be even better. I opened Owen's office. He'd purposefully left all his high-tech gear at home so he could "get back to nature" on his trip. I didn't think he'd mind if I borrowed his digital video camera. Or one of his digital video cameras, I should say. I had my choice of four. "Sweet!" I said, holding up a black camera as small as a credit card.

"Cool!" Lily said. "I didn't even know they made them that small."

"Here, you can use this one," I said. I handed her another camera that was about the size of a TV remote control.

"Okay, I'll use this huge one. But what am I doing with it?" Lily asked.

"We need to prove that Mimi Hansen is a big fat fake," I said. "No one will believe us. But if we can get some pictures of her factory, then maybe people will stop worshiping her."

"Wow! We solved our first case!" Lily said. We got on the elevator to go downstairs.

"Not yet. We know the answer to one part. But we still don't know who was stealing the paintings," I said.

"I thought it was Mr. Bike Messenger Guy," Lily said. "Ms. Murdoch's brother."

"I'm not so sure. I still think he can't be trusted, but I'm not sure how he fits in. What would his motive be?"

"Money? That's usually a pretty good motive," Lily said.

She had a point. But something still didn't seem quite right.

Our timing was perfect. We reached the black door to The Factory just as a couple of the guys we'd seen upstairs were heading back in. Their break must be over. I grabbed the door before it closed completely. We waited until the footsteps heading upstairs got softer and faded. We tiptoed up the stairs and back into the little closet. Drat! I was so used to taking Ruff everywhere that I still had him with me. The little guy was being especially mellow, as if he was trying to prove his worthiness for undercover work.

"Let's see if this works," I said. I put the viewfinder of the camera right up to the peephole and started videotaping. "Darn!" I had to suppress a laugh when I passed it to Lily to take a look. The camera had captured James's dreadlocks and half of Ms. Murdoch. "I don't suppose Mimi will be crouching down so I can get her head into a shot, will she?" I whispered. "Because this isn't the kind of video that makes good TV."

"I'll take care of it," Lily said. "But you have to give me the little cute camera. I've had enough of this monster."

Lily handed over the comparatively huge three-inch camera, and I reluctantly gave her the teensy tiny one. She looked at me intensely. "On second thought," she whispered, "this is your gig." She handed the miniature video camera back to me.

"Huh?" Oops. I hope I didn't say that too loudly. But as it turns out, we could probably be talking in normal voices and no one in The Factory would be able to hear us. Lily crossed her arms and sighed as if exasperated with me. "It's time, Hannah my dear, for you to go onstage. Now."

I knew she was right. Not about me acting, but about me getting to the bottom of this. If there was a bottom to be found, I was the one who was going to find it, and if I was lucky, I wouldn't end up on my own bottom. I put some Burt's Bees lip balm on my lips and did a silent smacking. I did a quick finger comb of my hair and then flipped it over my shoulder in what I hoped was a dramatic manner.

"Perfect!" Lily crooned. "Now go break a leg. But don't really break a leg or trip or do anything klutzy." Her confidence in me seemed to be waning.

She gently shoved me out of the closet and into the hallway. I took a deep breath and barged right through the door of The Factory. It was a showstopping entrance, if I do say so myself, yet no one even noticed me. The music was still loud, and all the artists were intensely working at their easels. Mimi was intently text messaging on her cell phone. Excellent. I could get some good shots before they noticed me.

I cupped Owen's tiny digital camera in the palm of my hand and started filming.

"Excuse me!" I called over the music. I waved my hands slowly over my head to get their attention. It was hard not to smile at my improvisational skills, since the hand-waving gesture was just to get some more video shots.

Mimi Hansen motioned for someone to turn down the music.

"You again! You seem to frequently appear in the wrong places," she said. "And this time, you have the wrong floor. This is a private workspace. Please leave."

"I'm sorry. I need help," I said. "I'm trying to find Nina Krimmel."

"Hannah?" Nina came out from behind an easel. "What are you doing here? How did you find me?" She turned to Mimi. "No one knew I was here. I didn't tell anyone, really."

Geesh. I hated to see Nina grovel.

"Nina!" I ran over to her. But I didn't take the most direct route. I wove my way through the room, passing paintings with the camera still cupped in my hand. "I'm so sorry," I said when I got to Nina. "I need your help. It's an emergency," she said.

"What's wrong? Are you okay? Is Maggie okay?" Nina looked genuinely worried. I must be pretty good at this acting thing.

"Yes! It's Maggie. AND Lily. And Billy Bob and Bobbie Joe, too," I said. Hey, I couldn't be expected to be totally original with names when I was improvising.

Nina looked at me like, *Huh, what the heck are you talking about?*

"You can't let outsiders into The Factory!" Mimi bellowed. "I don't know who this girl is or how she found you, but I can assure you that you are no longer creating Mimi Hansen art. Nor will you be paid for this evening's work."

"Oh, who cares!" Nina snapped. "Some things are more important than Mimi Hansen!"

"Right on, Nina!" I said. Oops. I forgot I was in the middle of an "emergency." I moved back into my sniveling role. "Nina, please, we need to go now." I started marching out of the workroom as if on a mission, but I wanted to get more video shots. The inspiring words of my acting coach, the great Lily Shannon, seeped into my head: *Break a leg. But don't really break a leg or trip or do anything klutzy.*

So I tripped.

CHAPTER 25

WHILE DOWN ON ALL FOURS, I READJUSTED THE CAMERA IN MY HAND and figured out how to stand back up while getting some more video.

"Oh, oh, oh! I'm so sorry. I'm so embarrassed. I just am just so worried about Bobbie Bill and Billy Joel," I said, all weepy.

"Don't you mean Billy Bob and Bobbie Joe?" Conner Murdoch asked.

"Give her a break!" Nina snapped. "Can't you see how upset she is? We need to get out of here. Come on, Hannah. We've got to get to Billy Joel and Billy Bob."

"Billy Bob and Bobbie Joe," Conner called after us.

"Whatever," I said.

Nina and I made a run for it.

Lily and Ruff met us in the hallway, and we charged down the two flights of stairs and out onto the sidewalk.

"Come on! Back to our apartment," I said.

• • •

We started sprinting. "You'd better tell me that everyone is okay," Nina panted.

"Mom and I are fine. We just wanted to get you out of there before anything happens," I said. "Sorry if I scared you too much."

"You were brilliant!" Lily said. "You've learned a lot from me, I must say."

"You had me going at first. Billy Bob and Bobbie Joe was a little over-the-top, but it got my attention," Nina said. "When we get upstairs, we're calling Maggie, and then you're telling both of us what's going on."

"I'm sorry if we blew it for you, Nina, but we wanted to get you out of there," I said.

"Why? Nothing dangerous was going on. I mean, I'm not proud of the fact that I've been painting pieces for Mimi Hansen to pass off as her own. But it wasn't like I was her prisoner or anything."

"I wanted you out because we took some video of what was going on inside The Factory," I said. "I'm going to call Mom and ask her to see if Mary Perez wants to look at it."

We got off the elevator, and I fumbled for the keys to the apartment.

"I don't know if it's exactly newsworthy that we're painting for someone else," Nina said. "It's not even illegal."

"It should be illegal!" I cried. "She's a big fake. It's fraud. People are paying her for things she didn't create. You're an artist, Nina! You deserve to have your name on your work, and you deserve recognition for your work. I can't stand Mimi Hansen getting all the credit for what other people have done."

"She won't be getting credit for long," a man's voice said.

Conner Murdoch was in the hallway, right behind us.

"I'll take that video you took while you were so concerned about your Billy Bob," Conner said.

"I don't know what you're talking about," Lily claimed. "Can't you see we're having a family emergency?"

"Get off it." Conner sneered. He pulled something from his bag. "Here, doggy. Come and get it." Ruff leaped toward whatever was inside the brown wrapper, and in one smooth motion Conner scooped up the pup and backed away from us.

"Give me your camera, and I'll give you the mutt."

"Ruff!" I lunged toward Conner, but he stuffed Ruff into his bag.

"Perhaps you didn't hear me. You give me the camera; I give you the dog."

"Why are you protecting Mimi Hansen? You should

want her to be exposed for the fake she is," I said, trying to not let a begging tone enter my voice. "Your own sister is being used."

"I'm not protecting Mimi anymore," he said with a hint of disgust, as if I was a total idiot for even thinking that.

"Conner, really, this is a bit extreme. I'm not sure yet if it's funny or embarrassing," Nina said. "For you, that is."

He dropped Ruff and left abruptly.

CHAPTER 26

"I NEED TO GET TO WIRED. I'M WORKING THE LATE SHIFT TONIGHT," Nina said. "What should I tell Maggie when I get there?"

"Never mind. I'm here," Mom called from the doorway of the apartment. "I couldn't get Hannah to answer her cell phone. I called you, Nina, to check on Hannah, but you didn't answer, either. I called the apartment and still no answer. Is everything okay?"

"The girls can explain. I really better get to work," Nina said. "I lost one job tonight. I can't afford to lose the other." I winced when she said that. "I'm kidding, Hannah. I hated working for Mimi. You know that," she said, giving me a quick hug before she left the apartment.

We filled Mom in on The Factory and who was there. "Look, we can show you," Lily said. We went to the computer and downloaded the video from Owen's camera.

"So the old marketing wizard runs an art factory, and then just puts her signature on other people's work?" Mom said. "It makes perfect sense. There was always something so artificial about the way Mimi talked about art. It didn't seem possible that one person could do so many paintings, let alone have such a wide variety of art styles."

"I'm pretty sure there's more to the story," I said. "I think Mimi arranged the thefts."

"This would be a great story for Mary Perez," Mom said.

"We could take her over to The Factory tonight, and she could pin down Mimi," I said.

Mary was at our apartment in twelve minutes. After she'd watched the video, we showed her the door to The Factory across the street. "Maybe I can get our own news crew in there tonight," she said. "Or maybe I need to be more covert. I think I'll go interview Mimi off camera."

"Good luck getting her to talk if there isn't a camera on her face," I said.

Lily and I stayed out on the balcony and watched Mary cross First Avenue. Lily had the binoculars focused toward The Factory door.

"It looks like something is up in the world of purple and black," Lily said.

Conner Murdoch and his bike were back at The Factory.

"What are you doing carrying the dog?" Lily panted as we ran out of Belltown Towers and onto the sidewalk.

"Well, I couldn't leave him in Owen's apartment. We're going to have to keep him with us," I said.

We were running without a plan. We crossed the street and headed toward the black door to The Factory.

"Aaarrrgggh!" Wouldn't you know it? I tripped again. I went sprawling down on the sidewalk. Ruff escaped from my arms.

"Ruff! Come!" I called as I tried to get up with a little bit of dignity.

Conner Murdoch was coming out the door with a rectangular flat package in his arms. He didn't even look in our direction. He just jumped on his bike and started pedaling.

Only he had a hitchhiker.

"Off! Get off!" he yelled.

But Ruff had gotten hold of his left sock, and it didn't look like the little terrier had any intention of letting go. Conner tried to pedal a few times.

Ruff clenched his little teeth tightly on Conner's

sock. There's no way that terrier was going to let go. Ruff just went around and around while Conner tried to pedal.

Crash!

Ruff was still hanging on.

Conner jumped off his bike and started running.

Ruff hung on.

Conner and Ruff made it only a few steps.

"Have a nice trip!" a voice called out. Suddenly Jordan Walsh was back in the action, sticking her leg out as if she were a third-grade bully.

"Conner!" Ms. Murdoch exclaimed as he tumbled to the ground. Mimi Hansen, Mary Perez, Mr. Snotty Art Guy, and James were right behind her. Ruff escaped the crowd and ran back to me.

"You again," Mr. Snotty Art Guy sneered his greeting to me.

"Jordan!" Mimi said. "I thought your father was picking you up."

"He's still running late," Jordan said in a somewhat blasé voice. "Am I interrupting something?"

"Conner, why did you take one of my paintings?" Ms. Murdoch asked her brother, looking down at the canvas that was peeking out from under the Kraft paper wrapping.

"That wasn't in the plans!" Mimi said, admonishing Conner. "Did you know about this?" She turned to Mr. Snotty Art Guy, who just shook his head.

"I did it for you," Conner said quietly to his sister. "I don't want you involved in any of this."

Mary Perez was looking from Mimi to Conner, who was still on the ground, as if deciding who to go after. I couldn't help myself. I had to butt in.

"The plans? You mean you knew what was going on all along? I knew it! You were stealing your own paintings!" I stared at Mimi. She didn't say anything. "Wait! Let me correct that. You were hiring people to create paintings that you passed off as your own, and then you tried to steal them?"

"Brilliant bit of publicity, wasn't it?" Conner Murdoch said, standing up and brushing himself off.

Mimi, the queen of publicity and TV interviews, seemed absolutely speechless now. Then she cleared her throat. "I'm sure I don't know what you're talking about," she said. "I'm ready to talk on TV now," she said to Mary. "I want to do all I can to help you break this story to get to the bottom of who was stealing Mimi Hansen paintings." She looked poised for a full TV interview now. You had to give her credit, she really recovered her public persona quickly.

"I have a few questions to ask you and the others before I ask you to comment on camera," Mary said. "Perhaps we could start upstairs with the artists' help in identifying their work."

"I would like to identify my work," James said.

"Conner, I don't know what's going on," Ms. Murdoch said to her brother. "But I think I'll go stand behind my work right now." She went upstairs, too.

"I have an idea how your mom can stand behind the artists' work—the real artists' work," I said to Jordan.

I headed upstairs with Jordan and the others. I figured if the proposal came from Mimi's daughter, and in front of witnesses, she'd have a harder time saying no. By the time I had explained it all to her, Jordan had a big smile on her face. This time, I could tell that it was sincere.

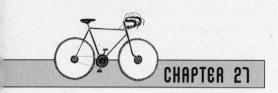

CHAPTER 27

AND THAT'S HOW WE ALL ENDED UP HERE AT THE FAIRMONT OLYMPIC Hotel. Lily, Mom, Nina, James, Ms. Murdoch, Jordan Walsh, Mary Perez, and me—all at our own table at the Honcho auction. Jordan even had her limousine pick us up for the ride over.

Sure, our table is in the back of the room close to the kitchen, but just getting in the door is $250 a head. We were here compliments of Mimi Hansen. That's right. Mimi Hansen bought us tickets—$2,000 for our seats— to the auction. And the best was yet to come.

"What did we miss?" Lily asked when she and Jordan got back from the bathroom.

"Let's see ... a dinner for two on a sailboat in Shilshole Bay Marina for twelve hundred and fifty dollars—and the boat isn't even going anywhere. A weekend at Whistler for four thousand fifty dollars. A glass bowl by one of Dale Chihuly's students for twelve thousand." I rattled off the prices. Mom and I were keeping track of each item in the hefty program.

"Are you kidding? Twelve grand for a bowl? I'd be afraid to eat my Frosted Mini-Wheats in a bowl that cost that much," Lily said.

"Don't worry," Jordan said. "You didn't buy it."

"You guys! This is the best part coming up," I said. I looked over at Nina and James. "I mean, this is the *second* best part coming up."

The tuxedoed auctioneer onstage boomed, "Ladies and gentlemen, this brings us to the canine portion of our evening, beginning with Willow!" A beautiful Weimaraner with clear blue eyes came onstage, accompanied by a woman in a sparkling gray gown that complemented Willow's coat. The dog stayed calm despite the applause. Bidding began at $1,500 and didn't stop until $8,000.

"I want to make sure Walker goes to a good home," I said, pointing out an entry in the program.

Walker came out onstage with a black velvet bow tie. "And here he is. A one hundred percent Shelter Special. All the dog you need in one package," the auctioneer said. "Let's start the bidding at one hundred dollars." That seemed a little insulting to Walker, who was an adorable medium-size mutt with a golden coat and white paws. Soon I had new respect for these Honcho folks, because there was passionate bidding for Walker. He seemed to know all the excitement was for him, because when bidding topped out at $9,500, he started barking.

Dorothy Powers was up onstage now. "It is my pleasure to introduce to you Mimi Hansen." Mimi, resplendent in a backless shimmering lavender gown and high-rise heels, hugged Dorothy as the crowd clapped enthusiastically.

"At this time, I'd like to unveil some of the greatest talent in art today," Mimi began. One of the spotlights hit our table as Mimi continued: "Nina Krimmel, Shelley Murdoch, and James Farnsworth. Tonight you have the rare opportunity to bid on these artists' work and then watch as they sign their work in front of you." The applause was deafening.

"I'm so nervous," Nina said. "What if no one bids?"

She needn't have worried. Bidding was fast and high, with each painting going for at least $15,000, including the one by Ms. Murdoch that Conner had attempted to steal and return to his sister. Everyone in the crowd rose to their feet as the artists from our table worked their way up to the stage to sign their paintings. Mimi had promised to pay each of them half of what each painting sold for as her "donation to the arts." Mom said it was guilt money, but Nina said it seemed cleaner to her than the $300 she would have gotten from Mimi for working at The Factory.

The artists working at The Factory had ended up on the Channel 4 News last weekend, and they'd stayed in the news all week. However, Mimi still emerged as the star in the public's eyes. She claimed the artists were working on pieces she'd commissioned for the auction and that there was no question that they would receive full credit for their work. That took care of the unsigned paintings, but she hadn't come up with a good scheme for the ones she'd actually signed. Mr. Chomsky, our upstairs neighbor, had been working on his own to trace who had actually created the paintings Mimi Hansen had claimed—and sold—as her own.

Speaking of Mr. Chomsky, I needed to get some footage of this part of the auction for him. Even with all the excitement of the auction and solving the Mimi mystery, he still wouldn't leave his apartment.

Conspicuously absent from this Mimi Hansen–loving crowd were Conner Murdoch and Mr. Snotty Art Guy. Conner had been delivering packages on the side to Mr. Chomsky. That turned out to be completely unrelated to the work he was doing for Mimi Hansen.

But Conner admitted that he'd delivered the blank canvas to Dorothy Powers as an attempt to show Mimi that she needed to watch out or he'd leak it to the press that she was orchestrating all the thefts, with his help and a gallery insider (Mr. Snotty Art Guy). Mary Perez was going to break that story after the auction.

It was all coming together quite nicely, I thought as I put Owen's tiny video camera away.

"Hannah, this was all such a great idea," Nina said. "I wish I could thank you."

"I think you've come up with a pretty decent way to help us out," Mom said. She passed her phone to me so I could read her text message: 436 Portage Bay, Dock 3.

"What's that?" I asked.

"That's our next address," Mom said. "Thanks to a customer at Wired that Nina met."

"It doesn't look like a real address to me."

"I assure you that it's quite real. In fact, I predict you'll be so happy living there you'll be walking on water," she said.

"Huh?"

"And sleeping on water," she added.

"Again, I say: Huh?"

"Oh brother, Hannah. You can put together all kinds of clues for this Mimi Hansen publicity stunt and art heist, and yet you can't read your own mother. Maggie is practically spoon-feeding clues to you. Walking on water. Portage Bay. Dock," Lily said. "You're going to be living . . ."

". . . on a houseboat!" I finished for her.

"Finally," Lily said with a big sigh. "For a smart girl, you can be kind of slow."

I decided to ignore Lily.

"Really, Mom? We're living on a houseboat?"

"Really, Hannah. We're going to live on Jake Heard's houseboat on Lake Washington."

"We're going to live on a houseboat!" I yelped.

"It will be wonderfully quiet," Mom said wistfully.

"I just hope it's not too dull," I said.

"I bet nothing strange ever happens on the tranquil waters of Lake Washington," Lily said.